SUBVERSIVE

THOEMMES

*To Marion, a most discerning
reader and a true feminist*

THE JOURNAL OF A FEMINIST

Elsie Clews Parsons

With a new Introduction and Notes by
Margaret C. Jones

THOEMMES PRESS

Published in 1994 by

Thoemmes Press
85 Park Street
Bristol BS1 5PJ
England

ISBN 1 85506 250 X

Warmest thanks to Dr Herbert Parsons, to David M. Parsons and
to Herbert Parsons Jr, for their generous permission to publish the
Journal manuscript; also to Miss Fanny Culleton for her consent to
reproduce photographs of Elsie Parsons; to Beth Carroll-Horrocks
of the American Philosophical Society in Philadelphia, who has
given me indispensable help in working on Parsons' writings long-
distance; and to Rachel Lee and Kate Docker of the Thoemmes
Press for their support for the *Journal* project. Above all, my deep
gratitude goes out to Marie Mulvey Roberts, indefatigable scholar
and generous editor, for her abiding faith in and encouragement
for this work.

Printed in Great Britain by Athenaeum Press Ltd.,
Newcastle-upon-Tyne.

INTRODUCTION

'Christian churchmen once debated the question whether or not women had souls, a controversy which now and again appears to be still unsettled.'[1]

The coiner of this sly aphorism is Elsie Clews Parsons, anthropologist, feminist, social critic, activist, wit, and conscious opponent of the stale and conventional. That her entertaining and original *Journal of a Feminist* has lain unpublished for the past eighty years is only slightly less surprising than that her crucial contributions to turn-of-century feminist thought have been so signally neglected in recent decades. Parsons may have decided not to publish *The Journal* for personal reasons, or owing to the pressure of work from her many other polemical and scholarly projects; but it is harder to understand why feminist works like *The Old-Fashioned Woman* and *Fear and Conventionality* have been overlooked, considering Parsons' influence on such diverse figures as Randolph Bourne, Ruth Benedict and H.L. Mencken,[2] not to mention the less readily determined effect of her articles in popular magazines, or of her lectures to clubs, to feminist groups, and to students at The New School for Social Research and at Columbia.

---

[1] *Religious Chastity: An Ethnological Study.* 1913. New York: AMS Press, 1975: p. 279.

[2] Bourne called Parsons' mind 'accurately modern in the...intellectual values that we most acutely need'. See 'A Modern Mind', his review of Parsons' *Social Rule* in *The Dial* 62 (1917): pp. 239–40.

For a discussion of Parsons' influence on Ruth Benedict, see Margaret M. Caffrey, *Ruth Benedict: Stranger in this Land*, Austin: University of Texas Press, 1989: pp. 96, 159, 185–98.

For H.L. Mencken's assessment see Peter Hare, *A Woman's Quest for Science: Portrait of Anthropologist Elsie Clews Parsons*, Buffalo, New York: Prometheus, 1985: p. 20.

Parsons earned her PhD from Columbia in 1899, and taught there from 1902 to 1905. She was a professional academic in an age when most young women of her class thought in terms of going 'into society' to pursue an eligible husband and a career of motherhood and social engagements. She was an anthropologist in the field, travelling unaccompanied in Ecuador and New Mexico when her female contemporaries shrank from a car journey with a male acquaintance unless another woman were present. She was one of the first lecturers at the New School for Social Research. She was president of the American Folklore Society (1918–1920), of the American Ethnological Association (1923–1925), and the first woman to be elected president of the American Anthropological Association (1940–1941). For twenty-three years she was associate editor of the *Journal of American Folklore*. She became a leading authority on the native Pueblo culture of the American Southwest. She also found time for active involvement in work for woman suffrage, for women's reproductive rights, and for anti-militarism.

Apart from her popular articles for *The Dial, The Independent, The New Republic and The Masses*, her more scholarly articles, and such anthropological studies as *Folklore from the Cape Verde Islands* and *Pueblo Indian Religion*, Parsons wrote six works for a more general readership, all of which to some extent address social issues from a feminist perspective. The publication of the first of these, *The Family* (1906), a study of marriage and parenting customs, caused something of a stir. In *The Family* Parsons declares her belief in monogamous relationships as 'conducive to emotional or intellectual development and health', but goes on to argue the desirability of 'early trial marriage, with a view to permanency, but with the privilege of breaking it if proved unsuccessful and in the absence of offspring without suffering any great deal of public condemnation'.[3] This, by

---

[3] *The Family: An Ethnographical and Historical Outline*. New York: Putnam's, 1906: pp. 348–49.

late-twentieth century criteria, not very drastic recommendation, caused violent controversy when *The Family* was published, reaching well beyond the book's few thousand readers. The idea of trial marriage was denounced in the press, but also employed as a legal defense by a man accused of elopement with a fifteen-year-old, who declared before the court that he had acted under the influence of Parsons' theories. The publicity caused political embarrassment to Elsie Parsons' husband Herbert, a Republican congressman, then chairman of the Republican Committee of New York County and a close political associate of President Theodore Roosevelt. Elsie Parsons sent Roosevelt a copy of *The Family* to reassure him as to the book's actual content, with a covering letter in which she promised, 'Henceforward in our family authorship is going to yield to statesmanship after as well as before elections'.[4]

Fortunately for us, Parsons did not honour this promise for long. However, she did publish her second book, *Religious Chastity* (1913), a meticulously detailed, sharply observant and often highly ironic study of ascetic practices in the religions of various cultures, under the pseudonym 'John Main'. *Religious Chastity* makes no recommendations for social reform – but like Parsons' other works of popular sociology and anthropology it is notable for its sly wit. 'The ascetic stores up merit for himself. He is a spiritual capitalist', Parsons tells us.[5] *The Old-Fashioned Woman* (1913) is remarkable for its interest in gender socialization (of which more in due course). *Fear and Conventionality* (1914), *Social Freedom* (1915) and *Social Rule* (1916) use anthropological findings to explore the limits to social reforms (including reforms beneficial to the progress of feminism) imposed by human fear of anomalies

---

[4] For an account of the controversy over the idea of 'trial marriage', see Hare, pp. 11–12. See also Rosemary Levy Zumwalt, *Wealth and Rebellion: Elsie Clews Parsons, Anthropologist and Folklorist*, Urbana and Chicago: University of Illinois Press, 1992: pp. 42–51, 86, 87, 112–13.

[5] *Religious Chastity*, p. 276.

and of change, or by individuals motivated by a will to power.

After the publication of *Social Rule* Parsons turned increasingly to work of a more specialized, scholarly nature – compilations of folklore from the Sea Islands off South Carolina and from the Cape Verde Islands, studies of Pueblo culture, like the monumental two-volume *Pueblo Indian Religion* (1939).

But it is her earlier, more popular work, with its independent and often highly original speculation about the nature and dynamics of social institutions which is most likely to be of abiding interest to the social critic, particularly to the feminist. *The Journal of a Feminist* belongs in this earlier group.

In the form of a first-person narrative purportedly written by a fictional character whose life and attitudes closely resemble those of Elsie Parsons herself, *The Journal* offers a concise and convenient introduction to many of the ideas Parsons covers with more scholarly detail in her other early writings. *The Journal* deals with gender socialization and women's fight for the vote, with reproductive rights and sexual freedom, with careers for women, approaches to parenting, the tyrannies of patriarchy and of gerontocracy, with militarism – all topics to which Parsons returns repeatedly in her published books and articles. To the social historian, moreover, *The Journal* offers a portrait of an early-twentieth century woman who, like her creator Elsie Parsons, inhabits several worlds – that of the wife and mother, that of the wealthy leisured society woman, that of the upper-class social activist and committee member, and those of the professional academic and the adventurous, well-travelled social scientist. *The Journal* is a source of information about customs of a past era – the chaperonage of women, legal bans on birth control information, taboos on women smoking or bathing without stockings – which do indeed seem to the late-twentieth century, as Parsons herself predicted they would, like the more arcane practices of even remoter ages.

Like her creator, the fictional diarist of *The Journal*, Cynthia, is perceptive, witty, and possessed of an insatiable curiosity. Cynthia is forever asking other people why they think and act as they do – especially in the case of those whose conservative attitudes she feels moved to criticize. Why, she asks her daughter Janet, does the father of Janet's friend Emma forbid the girls to ride round the family's estate when foreign labourers are working there? Why does a male lawyer of Cynthia's acquaintance resent the idea of a woman's practising law? From whence does an office manager employed by Cynthia's husband derive the right to police the private lives of his women employees? What connection exists between a tribal taboo and the widespread belief that a woman who votes or otherwise participates in politics will 'lose her femininity'? Cynthia's questions – and Cynthia's answers – spare no-one – not even Cynthia herself, as the narrator's observations are further dissected in footnotes by that erudite and sceptical ethnologist, 'E.C.P.'

'E.C.P.' writes an Introduction for Cynthia's *Journal*, in which she claims to have given Cynthia the inspiration for *The Journal* in the first place. She gives the reader a brief biography of Cynthia which, like the portrait of the narrator which emerges from the *Journal* as a whole, bears an obvious resemblance to the life and opinions of Elsie Clews Parsons. However, 'Cynthia' and 'E.C.P.' sometimes appear to represent two alternative views of a topic on which Parsons herself had not made up her mind. Thus, for instance, Cynthia argues that when a man refers facetiously to his wife as 'the head of the house' he does so only because he is aware that she is nothing of the kind – that her domestic position is that of a subordinate and inferior. 'E.C.P' tells Cynthia flatly, '...you're quite wrong, Cynthia. Such terms may be mere circumlocutions to avoid naming a wife – or a husband.'[6] Or 'E.C.P.' derides as 'doctrinaire' Cynthia's declaration that sexist attitudes can be eliminated by mere intellectual persuasion.[7] Whatever

[6] *The Journal*, p. 75.

[7] *The Journal*, p. 72.

Parsons' own reasons for the introduction of this dialogue between diarist and editor, the divergences of opinion of the two personae act for the reader as a safeguard against complacency. Readers are forced to take sides.

Another function of the notes by 'E.C.P.' is to set early-twentieth century Western cultural practices within an anthropological context. She defamiliarizes and demystifies Western beliefs and customs by showing them as part of cultural patterns shared in common with societies to which Europeans and European-Americans of Parsons' day liked to think themselves superior. Thus, the Western taboo on nakedness is found to be shared with the Melanesians of New Guinea. 'Stag parties' are a manifestation of male resistance to eating in company with women which is also found among the native people of Hawaii. Like people of Western European descent in the United States, some groups of native Americans manifest contemptuous attitudes towards unmarried older women.

Parsons' fearless insistence on defamiliarization of accepted social practices is an attitude to be internalized by anyone wishing to contribute to the development of a more rational and just social order. And *The Journal* employs this technique of defamiliarization to grapple with issues which for us in the late-twentieth century still have not lost their controversial aspects. Women's reproductive rights; the rights of children and of adults within marriage; social attitudes towards sexually contracted diseases; consumerism and the conditioning of women and children as consumers; the burdens imposed on women by the nuclear family on one hand and the competitive nature of the labour market on the other, are all concerns discussed in Parsons' work which we can recognize as relevant to our own late-twentieth century society. Above all, *The Journal* explores the vexed question of relations between the sexes in a world where women experience domination by male power. Whether lesbian or heterosexual, women have still to engage the question Cynthia formulates: 'How are women to live *with* men, not *without* men like the ruthless fighters for institutional freedom, and not in the old way

through men.' Interesting work and a lifesyle involving
enough periods of physical separation from the 'significant
other' to avoid 'the unbroken familiarity of bed and board'
which leads to staleness and dependency are Parsons'
tentative solutions.[8] Far from declaring the discussion
closed, however, Cynthia's speculative approach invites her
readers to engage for themselves the issues she raises – if
possible, to contribute their own answers to her questions.

Apart from anything else, *The Journal* is immensely
enjoyable to read, full of wit and humour and radiating
that quality in Parsons' writing her friend Randolph Bourne
called 'a fine adventurous command of life'.[9] Parsons'
character Cynthia is a sardonic observer – and a careful
listener. With an acute ear for dialogue Cynthia records
the irritable conversation of a middle-aged married couple
on a train – 'Be careful, you'll tip backwards dear' – in
which the expressions of concern for one another are
clearly the thinnest of pretexts for a clash of wills.[10] Or she
notes the testy reiterations of an elderly senator who
repeatedly declares, 'Anyhow, I'm against suffrage' for
women, but finds himself unable to articulate exactly
why.[11] She captures the insecurity felt by a lawyer whose
profession has just begun to be 'invaded' by women. He
would avoid working with a woman lawyer, he says, as he
would run from 'a woman who raised a cane to me in the
street'.[12] Unsparing of others as she is, however, Cynthia is
also capable of telling stories against herself. After she has
held forth to an older woman (a character loosely based on
Parsons' own mother) on a refusal to wear restrictive
clothing as one aspect of feminist rebellion – 'When I took
off my veil or gloves whenever your back was turned or

[8] *The Journal*, p. 46.

[9] Quoted in Eric Sandeen, 'Bourne Again: the Correspondence Between Randolph Bourne and Elsie Clews Parsons', *American Literary History*, Fall 1989: pp. 489–509.

[10] *The Journal*, p. 26.

[11] *The Journal*, p, 98.

[12] *The Journal*, p. 82.

when I stayed in my room for two days rather than put on stays, that was feminism' – Cynthia finds that her peroration has had unexpected results:

> The following day the lady sent Janet [Cynthia's daughter] the white kid gloves and the gauze veil that Janet had asked her for – 'because Mother won't buy them for me'. I suppose our colloquy had reminded her...[13]

Like her creator, Parsons' character Cynthia shows an ability to get on with people of very diverse backgrounds. In her relations with others Cynthia illustrates effectively what Parsons celebrated as 'a love of personality', a gift for appreciating the specific qualities of each individual she encounters. This love of personality is apparent in, for example, Cynthia's friendship with Mr Clack of Gallup, her driver and guide through the hills of New Mexico, who thinks Cynthia 'the most romantic woman he has ever met', and presents her with a bottle of beer as a parting gift.[14] It manifests itself in Cynthia's conspiracy with a friendly train conductor who lets her smoke on the train in contravention of the ban on 'ladies'' smoking in US railroad cars.[15] It shows itself again in Cynthia's remarks on a young girl at a women's peace parade, whose obvious enjoyment of the event and her role in it in turn give Cynthia pleasure;[16] or in a discussion with a socialist/feminist student whose radicalism Cynthia finds hopelessly unrealistic, but with whom she makes common cause against the sexist conservatism of Cynthia's husband Amos.[17]

Love for personality is also a keynote in Cynthia's accounts of her attempts to answer the endless questions of her daughter Janet, about divorce laws, about 'fairness' in competition, about the usefulness of her mother's taking

[13] *The Journal*, p. 84.

[14] *The Journal*, pp. 26–27.

[15] *The Journal*, p. 14.

[16] *The Journal*, p. 100.

[17] *The Journal*, pp. 71–72.

part in a 'peace parade'. Janet shows herself to be somewhat more of a social conservative than her mother – a difference which Cynthia on the whole accepts. 'My sceptical daughter', she calls Janet, when Janet questions the usefulness of the peace parade. It is a term which gently satirizes – but which also seems to respect her daughter's stubborn independence of mind, a trait Janet shares with her mother.[18]

Elsie Parsons was born in November 1874, into the family of Henry Clews, a wealthy self-made man, the son of a Staffordshire potter, who became the well-known founder of a New York banking firm. Her mother was Lucy Madison Worthington Clews of Kentucky, a descendant of President James Madison and the granddaughter of Gabriel Slaughter, governor of Kentucky. Elsie Parsons was the eldest of three children, and the only daughter.

From an early age, Elsie showed rebellious tendencies that seem to have made her both a trial and something of a puzzle to her conservative, fashion-conscious mother. Cynthia's description of her teenage refusal to wear stays, veils or gloves, is closely based on Elsie's own. This unconventionality in dress Parsons was to adopt at intervals throughout her adult life, walking hatless in the street, or wearing tennis shoes with a formal gown. She also liked to sit with the men after dinner, instead of 'retiring' with the women; and she disliked and avoided all such conventional greetings as 'goodbye', or 'Merry Christmas'. She also disliked thank you letters, funerals and weddings. Much against the wishes of her mother, who had expected her daughter to groom herself for a 'coming out' in fashionable society, Elsie attended and graduated from Barnard College, and went on to earn her PhD from Columbia. As she herself suggests in *The Journal of a Feminist*, her interest in anthropology, which evolved out of her initial interests in education and in sociology, was not unconnected with this early sense of

[18] *The Journal*, p. 101.

contrast between what her family expected of her socially, and what she observed as the differing cultural norms of others – of, for example, the working class children with whom, much against her mother's wishes, she ran off to play in the public parks.[19] As a friend described Parsons, in terms which allude playfully to her vocation as an anthropologist:

> ...she wears the usual tribal adornments and bead-work and skins, and she sleeps and eats in the family's big stone igloo near Fifth Avenue.... But every now and then her neglect of some small ceremonial sets the whole tribe to chattering about her, and eying her closely, and nodding their hairy coiffures or their tall shiny hats, whispering around their lodge fires, evenings, that Elsie is queer.[20]

Despite her theoretical and practical social independence (an independence underwritten, one should not forget, by immense inherited wealth) she made a suprisingly conventional marriage. Herbert Parsons, five years her elder, was a New York lawyer, an active Republican, who was to serve three terms as a congressman, and who from 1905 to 1910 was chairman of the Republican Committee of New York County. He was a conservative upholder of tradition where Elsie was an iconoclast. While she was a pacifist and an opponent of militarism, he was a traditional nationalist. Apart from the attraction she felt towards Herbert Parsons – an attraction strong enough to enable her to overcome her initial resistance to the idea of marriage as an institution – Elsie Parsons retained an abiding love and affection for him. Not surprisingly, however, there were periods of estrangement, engendered by disagreements over the proper upbringing of their four children, over Herbert Parsons' decision to volunteer to serve in the First World War, and over the extramarital affairs in which both Herbert and Elsie engaged.[21]

---

[19] *The Journal*, pp. 4–5, 84.

[20] Clarence Day, Jr, 'Portrait of a Lady', *New Republic*, 23 July 1919: pp. 387–89.

[21] For an account of the relationship of Elsie Parsons with her husband see Zumwalt, pp. 55–97.

For all the conventionality of her married life, in her pursuit of a career and above all in the independence of her intellect, Parsons is representative of the so-called New Woman of the turn of the century, one of a vanguard minority who were earning PhDs and entering traditionally masculine professions in ever-growing numbers.[22] She met others who shared her intellectual background and interests in the Greenwich Village women's club Heterodoxy, the sole condition for membership of which was that a woman should hold unorthodox views. The participants in this club were, according to Parsons' friend the writer and society hostess Mabel Dodge Luhan, women 'who did things and did them openly...fine, daring, rather joyous and independent women'.[23] At Heterodoxy, Parsons would have made the acquaintance of the social critic and reformer Charlotte Perkins Gilman, of radical activists and labour organizers like Rose Pastor Stokes and Elizabeth Gurley Flynn, of writers Inez Irwin, Helen Hull and Mary Heaton Vorse, and of Rheta Childe Dorr, editor of the National Woman's Party magazine, *The Suffragist*.[24] Though their definitions of feminism varied widely, all these women considered themselves in some sense feminists. All of them of course supported the fight for women's right to vote. A crucial difference in their views lay in the degree of faith they placed in attainment of the suffrage as a means of transforming society. For Rheta Childe Dorr, for instance, winning of the vote would guarantee a better society for women and men alike. When women entered political life they would eliminate slums and sweat shops and malnutrition, making of society one 'great, well-ordered, comfortable sanitary household'. The writer-

---

[22] For further information on this subject, a useful source is Nancy Cott's *The Grounding of Modern Feminism*, New Haven: Yale University Press, 1987.

[23] See Mabel Dodge (Luhan), *Movers and Shakers*, 1936. Albuquerque, New Mexico: University of New Mexico Press, 1985: pp. 143–44.

[24] For further information on Heterodoxy, see Judith Schwartz, *Radical Feminists of Heterodoxy: Greenwich Village, 1912–1940*, Lebanon, New Hampshire: New Victoria Publishers, 1982.

activist Mary Heaton Vorse, on the other hand, was later to express her disillusionment concerning similar hopes. It puzzled her that women should have been willing to fight and suffer to win the right to vote, 'unless they had a further imperative objective – the protection of all children, for instance, or an equal passion for peace...'.[25]   Parsons, never subscribed to the illusion that women's achievement of the vote would alone liberate women.   She knew that feminism would have to take account of the sociopsychological factors contributing to women's oppression. Writing from a perspective which remarkably anticipates the philosophy of the women's liberation movement of the early 1970s she writes in *The Journal of a Feminist*, '...feminists have been so impressed by the institutional bondage of women, by their disqualifications as property holders, as parents, as citizens, that questions of inner freedom have rarely occurred to them'.   Parsons offers examples of what she has in mind: 'checks upon going out alone, clothes that hinder movement, censorship of ideas and feeling, endless little sex taboos.'[26]   For Parsons, a basic precondition for women's freedom from the constraints of patriarchy is a questioning and reformulation of the very conception of gender. What this meant in terms of her understanding of feminism she spells out in detail in *The Journal of a Feminist*:

> This morning perhaps I may feel like a male; let me act like one.   This afternoon I may feel like a female; let me act like one.   At midday or at midnight I may feel sexless; let me therefore act sexlessly.   Even nowadays women resent having always to act like women, or to be treated invariably as women....

[25] See Dorr, *What Eight Million Women Want*, Boston: Small, 1910: p. 328; Vorse, *A Footnote to Folly: the Reminiscences of Mary Heaton Vorse,* New York: Farrar, 1935: p. 169.

[26] *The Journal*, p. 89.

'Some day,' Parsons adds, 'there may be a 'masculism'
movement to allow men to act 'like women.'[27] The dictum
'the personal is the political' would have needed no
explanation for Parsons.

As Parsons also remarks, the code of 'chivalry', feudal
and patriarchal in origin, ostensibly designed to protect
women and members of supposedly inferior social classes,
is actually a barrier erected against members of these
disadvantaged groups: 'It keeps them most rigorously and
most subtly in their place.'[28] The delimiting of women's
'proper' social role by patriarchal social conventions
directly affected Parsons in her professional life, as when,
for example, the male directors of the Santa Fe Laboratory
in Anthropology in the late 1920s consistently excluded
women researchers from their summer research groups and
field trips.[29] Less seriously perhaps, it must all the same
have been galling to have been told, during her student
years, by those who evidently regarded her as a freak of
nature, 'I hear you are so *literary*, Miss Clews'. This was,
Parsons recalls, 'the rather curious formula most commonly
used to put me in my place...'.[30] One can only speculate
about her reaction to finding herself introduced in *The
Independent* magazine, for which she had written an
erudite article on marriage and parenting, as 'the daughter
of Henry Clews, the well-known New York banker, and
the wife of Congressman Herbert Parsons'.[31]

Parsons' ethnological training made her acutely sensitive
to the ways in which children are socialized into gendered
behaviour at a very early age. She may well have been the
first Western social analyst to observe that children's
language in Western society shows the influence of social
conceptions of gender: '[A]re not 'lovely', 'darling',

[27] *The Journal*, p. 90.

[28] *Fear and Conventionality*, New York: Putnam's, 1914: p. 76.

[29] See Zumwalt, pp. 13–14.

[30] *The Old-Fashioned Woman: Primitive Fancies about the Sex*. 1913.
New York: Arno Press, 1972: p. 285.

[31] In *The Independent*, 18 Jan. 1906: pp. 146–47.

'sweet', 'horrid', 'mean', peculiarly girls' adjectives, and 'bully', 'fine', 'jolly', 'rum', 'rotten', 'bum', peculiarly boys'?'[32]   Parsons also anticipates the work of later feminist sociologists and linguists when she observes that 'Women use more colour terms than men – at least in the United States'.[33]   And she understands the connection between command of a particular terminology and the exclusiveness of power when she writes that, for men, the use of 'profane' language is 'a prerogative they safeguard by not even availing themselves of it before a woman'. Political terms, Parsons adds, have not yet been demystified by enough women's access to the vote to 'deprive men of the pleasure of explaining them to women'.[34]

Parsons is also sensitive to the ways in which patriarchal religious and social mores prescribe for, monitor and inhibit feminine behaviour.   Her article for *The Independent* of February 1912 examines the use in different cultures of supernatural sanctions which have the effect of preventing women from straying, either physically or psychologically, too far from home. Among native Australians, Parsons explains, a fear of evil spirits performs this function. Similarly, 'In the Niger Delta the Ibo impersonation of the dead has a right to any girl he can catch'. Other cultures have supernatural means whereby a husband can tell if a wife has been unfaithful. Among European-Americans, morevoer, as Parsons points out, men encourage their daughters to attend church, and until quite recently have discouraged them from attending college, for fear higher education will dilute the wholesome restraining effects of supernatural sanctions.[35]

Socially inculcated shame about female physiology is another effective inhibitor of women's independence which Parsons explores in her work. As she explains in *The*

---

[32] *Old-Fashioned Woman*, p. 159.

[33] *Old-Fashioned Woman*, p. 159

[34] *Old-Fashioned Woman*, pp. 152–54

[35] 'The Supernatural Policing of Women', *The Independent*, 8 Feb. 1912: pp. 307–10.

Journal of a Feminist, she herself felt no embarrassment
about walking naked in the house while her children were
present[36] – but her post-Victorian contemporaries for the
most part felt very differently about the female body. As
an illustration of contemporary social attitudes to the then
largely taboo subject of pregnancy, for instance, Parsons
tells in *The Old-Fashioned Woman* how a pregnant friend,
accustomed to more relaxed European attitudes, who went
out to dine in Washington society became the subject of
scandal.[37] Menstruation was another taboo subject, one
imbued, moreover, with a superstitious masculine dread of
woman as 'other' which imposed on women an obligation
to behave publicly as if the phenomenon did not exist. As
Parsons points out in *The Old-Fashioned Woman,* this
deceit is not without social consequences for the woman,
who must strive to 'act normally in every way'. Such
'normality' not only forces a woman often to 'endure
exraordinary discomfort and pain', but by her subterfuges
to give 'the impression of being generally unreliable'.[38]

The limitations placed on the expression of feminine
sexuality result in external constraints on women's freedom
of movement, but even more significantly, in an internal-
ization of those constraints by women themselves. For
every turn-of-century New Woman there were, as Parsons
points out, thousands of 'Old-Fashioned women' (Parsons'
own term) who were signally unadventurous in their
attitudes to life. As Parsons writes in *Fear and
Conventionality,*

> Rarely...do women go off by themselves – into the
> corner of a ballroom, into the wilderness, to the play,
> to the sacred high places of the earth or to the
> Islands of the Blessed. Penelope stays at home....[39]

[36] *The Journal,* p. 25.

[37] *Old-Fashioned Woman,* p. 83.

[38] *Old-Fashioned Woman,* p. 9.

[39] *Fear and Conventionality,* p. 49.

xx Introduction

Parsons' own attitudes and behaviour were, it goes without saying, very far from corresponding to this description. Her anthropological field work took her to the Sea Islands off South Carolina, to New Mexico, Mexico, Ecuador and the Cape Verde Islands. (She also travelled to the Philippines and Japan with her husband, who was part of a diplomatic and trade delegation for the Roosevelt administration.) When she travelled alone she was sometimes irked by the anxiety of others to shield her from the anticipated consequences of her solitary wanderings. On a visit to New Hampshire to observe an election there, the local people were amazed to find 'a lady' travelling unaccompanied.[40] On a field trip to South Carolina, Parsons was forced to escape from her overprotective hosts in order to be able to collect material at all.[41]

An essential factor in women's attainment of psychological independence – of 'spiritual independence', in Parsons' terminology, is of course their economic independence. Against the conviction of the anti-feminist that a woman's place lay in the home, Parsons argued that a career for a woman actually enhances the quality of family life, by the independence and self-respect it makes possible for the woman. The right kind of work for a woman can be, she writes in The Journal of a Feminist, 'a means of salvation for love'.[42] Having adopted this position, however, Parsons finds herself compelled to grapple with the further all-too-familiar issues raised by the conflict, in a free market system, between the demands of parenting and those of the workplace in which a woman is obliged to market her labour power. Parsons' solution – her recommendation that part-time employment be made available for working mothers – though innnovative when Parsons first proposed it, has since proved to disadvantage women rather than to empower them. However, she does make what for the 1900s were radical recommendations

[40] Old-Fashioned Woman, p. 294.

[41] Day, 'Portrait of a Lady', pp. 387–89.

[42] The Journal, p. 47.

(recommendations, for that matter, not yet implemented today). She calls for the provision of childcare facilities for working mothers, and of facilities where working mothers can breastfeed their babies. The latter, she contends, will never be provided as long as a 'lactation taboo' persists, whereby breastfeeding is regarded as a necessarily furtive act. Above all, she argues, a working mother's work 'must be accommodated to her nursing', rather than the reverse.[43]

Just as 'spiritual independence' and 'a love of personality' are the keys to Parsons' oft-repeated stress on women's rights to education and a career, so she defends the rights of both women and the young against a traditional society which privileges the conservative values of the elderly. She distrusts members of the older generation for the power they wield over the young – not least where the policing of sexuality is concerned.

She argues, for instance, that parents should have no rights to give or withhold consent to their children's marriages, even when the children are still minors.[44] The 'age-class', as Parsons calls it, of the older generation, has in her view no right to control the desires of a younger generation, whose interests and needs it cannot share. Unfortunately, in her view, as she expresses it in *The Journal of a Feminist*, 'the control of sex has always been in the hands of those free from its urgencies. It is indeed a government without representation, and of conditions far more significant for us than any condition politically determined.' She adds, 'The old are hard and make life hard. Some day we shall cease to sentimentalize over them and keep them in the place they deserve'.[45]

Women's cultural and legal rights in marriage and divorce are another focus of Parsons' feminism. Although she does not hesitate to declare heterosexual monogamy the ideal form in human sexual relations – a tenet that later

[43] 'Penalizing Marriage and Child-Bearing', *The Independent*, 18 Jan. 1906: pp. 146–47.

[44] See Hare, p. 91.

[45] *The Journal*, p. 64.

feminists may find more than a trifle problematic – she deplores 'the spirit of monopoly' which enters the marital relationship 'when marriage becomes frankly proprietary'.[46] While denouncing the absurdly restrictive divorce and 'breach of promise' laws of her day for the misery they cause, Parsons also stresses the futility of trying by institutional means to arrest the changes which are inevitable in all human relationships. Unfortunately, she argues, the human fear of 'impermanence' is such that 'Society' will have people remain legally attached to one another 'at any price, even at the price of sincerity, even at the price of all that makes the relationship worthy'.[47] As we have seen, Parsons proposes as an alternative 'early trial marriage', the substitution for divorce courts of 'parents' courts', and the signing by parents of a contract with the state in which one or both of them would undertake to raise their children. While parenthood, according to this theory, would remain a public concern subject to the intervention of the state on behalf of the child, the sexual relationship would otherwise be reserved as a purely private matter.[48]

Another area in which Parsons asserts women's rights against the claims of a patriarchal society is that of women's control over their own reproduction. Parsons is very much of her time in her interest in eugenics – and unfortunately, while democratic and egalitarian in so much of her thinking on social issues in general, imbued in her thought on eugenics with some of the elitism of that movement. One of her reasons for deploring the childlessness of unmarried women teachers, for example, is that she believes such women 'belong to a superior [intellectual] stock; and to penalize marriage and child-bearing for them is a crime against eugenics'.[49] On the

---

[46] *Religious Chastity*, p. 278.

[47] 'Feminism and Sex Ethics', *International Journal of Ethics*, July 1916: p. 464.

[48] In 'Marriage and Parenthood: A Distinction', *International Journal of Ethics* 25 (1915): pp. 514–17.

[49] 'Penalizing Marriage and Child-Bearing', p. 146.

other hand, she satirized those xenophobic social commen-
tators who feared that the Anglo-Saxon race in the United
States would fail to breed rapidly enough to continue
numerically and culturally to dominate the multi-ethnic
immigrant population. Such prophets of 'race suicide',
Parsons wrote,

> will talk to you about the high cost of living,
> pampered wives, nationality, or the god of an alien,
> ancient race, all facts, more or less…but none holding
> any relation whatsoever to the emotion of regret over
> the fallen birthrate which always warms up the speaker's
> peroration.…

In this article, 'Facing Race Suicide', published in *The
Masses* for June 1915, Parsons shows a clear appreciation
of the restrictive and oppressive conditions which made
some middle-class women reluctant to undertake a life of
domesticity and childrearing after their college education
had seemed to promise them a wider sphere of action.
They were, she wrote, 'taught to seek self-expression and
then denied it'. She concludes patronizingly, however, that
as long as such restrictions obtain, the prophets of race
suicide should be content to have the birthrate maintained
by 'those immigrants whose peasant education is consistent
with the conditions for mating and child-bearing obtaining
in America'.[50]
  In more enlightened vein, Parsons maintains, in
'Penalizing Marriage and Child-bearing', that so-called
'race-suicide' would be infinitely preferable to 'an only
child custom or a flourishing system of foundling
asylums'.[51] In her firm insistence that women's rights to
control their own reproduction should take precedence
over all other considerations she shows herself at her most
committedly feminist.
  On birth control and abortion Parsons was radical for
her time, and aware of how these issues affected society's

[50] 'Facing Race Suicide', *The Masses,* June 1915: p. 15.
[51] 'Penalizing Marriage and Child-Bearing', p. 147.

working-class majority. Access or lack of access to an abortion constituted, as she argues in *The Journal of a Feminist*, 'the crassest of class distinctions', since poor women were unable to gain assistance which upper-class women obtained easily.[52] It was this knowledge, and a comparable awareness and concern about the legal bans on disseminating birth control information which made of Parsons an activist on reproductive rights issues. She was among a group of intellectuals and activists who defended the birth control advocate Margaret Sanger in 1915 and 1916, when Sanger was prosecuted for giving birth control information to working-class patients in her New York clinic. At a pre-trial dinner at the Brevoort Hotel, it was Parsons who proposed that twenty-five women who had themselves used contraceptives should stand up in court with Margaret Sanger and declare themselves guilty of breaking the law. (Only one, however, volunteered.)[53] In *The Journal of a Feminist* Parsons' narrator Cynthia advocates a similar strategy in connection with the abortion issue, proposing that a doctor should be found who is willing to challenge the law by performing abortions for women in need, and that a group of concerned citizens be formed to back him during the inevitable ensuing prosecution. The doctor is understandably reluctant to take Cynthia's advice, given the stiff criminal penalties, not to mention the professional stigma, such a stand would incur. Instead, he expresses a wish that the American Medical Association or similar professional body would interest itself in the abortion and birth control issues.[54]

She could be satirical of the anti-feminist, or even of the non-feminist, the cautiously conservative 'old-fashioned woman', as she called her. In *The Journal of a Feminist* she writes of a wife and mother who seems to have read no books, seen no plays, attended no exhibitions, and who is

[52] *The Journal*, p. 81.

[53] For an account of Parsons' proposal, see the *Autobiography* of Margaret Sanger, New York: Norton, 1938.

[54] *The Journal*, p. 81.

less knowledgeable about current affairs than her ten-year-old daughter, so engrossed is she in bringing up her children. Still, Parsons' tone in portraying such women is less one of malice than of humorous exasperation.[55] As she writes of the suffragist who, despite her theoretical feminism, refuses to drive in a car with a male acquaintance unless she is chaperoned, 'Women will be women – in spite of suffrage'.[56] Women as socialized in a post-Victorian culture, one assumes Parsons means. As suggested earlier, Parsons' background in anthropology made her very well aware that various cultures construct gender very differently.

Her professional knowledge offers her a perspective from which to criticize stereotypes and prejudices in her native culture, including those related to gender. From this comparative standpoint she is enabled, for example, to understand in terms of a fear of anomalies and of difference to be found in many cultures the European-American view in which 'a girl not quite a girl' may be pejoratively named 'a tomboy, mannish, or, in milder terms, a bachelor maid'.[57] In another of her anthropological articles she describes the practice of cross-dressing among the Pueblo native Americans of Zuni – a socially accepted practice which Parsons observes to perform a number of functions. She explains that in Pueblo culture, 'Towards adolescence and sometimes in later life, it is permissible for a boy culturally to change sex. He puts on woman's dress, speaks like a woman, and behaves like a woman.' Parsons explains, a man may make this change because he prefers women's work ('because he wanted to work like a woman') or because 'his household was short of women and needed a woman worker'. As she remarks, 'This native theory of the institution of the man-woman is a curious commentary...on that thorough-going belief in the intrinsic

[55] *The Journal*, pp. 83–84.

[56] *The Journal*, p. 100.

[57] 'The Aversion to Anomalies', *Journal of Philosophy, Psychology and Scientific Method*, 15 April 1915: p. 213.

difference between the sexes which is so tightly held to in our own culture'.[58] In another article on Zuni definitions of gender published twenty years later, Parsons expresses regret that European influences are gradually eliminating the practice of transvestism in Zuni society – and hence, one presumes, a cultural difference which gives the lie to essentializing stereotypes and prescriptive definitions of gender.[59]

Parsons' interest in Pueblo child-rearing practices in her later anthropological work represents, as Franz Boas notes, a preoccupation with 'the influence of cultural forms upon personalities, the way in which personalities similar to those found in our own civilization respond to the demands of their culture'.[60] It is in the context of this interest in the effect of socialization upon the character that Parsons' previously cited 'love of personality' may better be understood – an interest in the pressures towards conformity which all cultures bring to bear upon the individual. She studied various cultures' collective anxieties about 'anomalies', about the unfamiliar, unusual or 'different': twins, the unmarried, the recently bereaved, woman who smoked, or woman who campaigned to vote. In her concern about the negative effects of social conformity based upon the fear of anomalies, she celebrated variability to the point where it became a veritable cult for her. The interest of Western societies of the 1990s in ethnic and multicultural diversity would have been a welcome phenomenon to Parsons – except that she would have wished to extend the celebration of difference to include a multitude of unclassifiable varieties of individual, personal behaviour.

Although Parsons uses the unfortunate cultural epithets of her day – 'savage' and 'primitive' – for people of non-

---

[58] 'Waiyautitsa of Zuni, New Mexico', *Scientific Monthly*, Nov. 1919: pp. 443–57.

[59] 'The Last Zuni Transvestite', *American Anthropologist* 41 (1939): pp. 338–40.

[60] A point discussed in Franz Boas' obituary for Parsons, 'Elsie Clews Parsons', published in *Science*, 23 Jan. 1942: pp. 89–90.

industrial cultures, her analyses in practice constantly undercut and deconstruct these categories. To begin with, she questions the Anglo-Saxon notions of northern European ethical/moral superiority deeply ingrained in the racist ethnology of the Eurocentric science of the period; for example in her celebration of the civilized collective ethos of Pueblo peoples. She finds in Pueblo culture 'a system not unworthy the attention of those who would unite happiness and contentment with labour', and in the Pueblo Hopi adage, 'Because any time any one may need help, therefore all help one another', a philosophy of 'realistic mutual helpfulness' from which European-American society can learn. She writes, 'That the Missionary or Trader should feel that he has superior goods or methods to offer the people on the mesa is matter, surely, for the God of Laughter or the grimmer God of Irony'.[61] Parsons appreciates, too, the will to power which motivates much discourse about 'the humbleness of so-called savage culture'. She views this 'will-to-power, the desire to have people like yourself or to have them amenable to immediate group ends' as 'well exemplified' in the official policies toward foreigners of early twentieth-century America – 'in the current movement for Americanization or in bureaus of immigration or Colonial or foreign offices'.[62] As a possible antidote to chauvinistic and xenophobic policies, Parsons calls for anthropologists to 'really study and understand cultural variation' and for policy makers to learn not only 'tolerance for group differences' but also 'appreciation of their value'.[63]

As an anthropologist in the field, Parsons herself did not always respect the rights of the cultural 'other'. She angered some members of the Taos Pueblo community when her scientific curiosity led her to violate the secrecy of Pueblo

[61] *A Pueblo Indian Journal, 1920-1921*. Menasha, Wisconsin: American Anthropological Association, 1925: p. 10.

[62] 'The Teleological Delusion', *Journal of Philosophy, Psychology and Scientific Method*, Aug. 1917: p. 466.

[63] 'The Study of Variants,' *Journal of American Folklore*, April–June 1920: pp. 87–90.

religious rites by publishing her findings.[64]   However, she had found sufficient acceptance among Pueblo peoples to be able to intervene on their behalf when the greed of white speculators threatened them. With her friend Mabel Dodge she was active in a successful campaign against the federal Bursum Bill of 1922 which would, if it had passed, have deprived Pueblo people of sixty thousand acres of land and given the land to white settlers. The fight against the bill represented the first national campaign to protect native American land rights in US history.[65]

As mentioned earlier, Parsons' background in anthropology does provide her with valuable insights, and valuable strategies, in developing her feminist arguments – as when she illustrates the pervasiveness of masculine assumptions of superiority to women, for example, by a discussion of the ways in which women's worth in financial terms is assessed in very different societies, but resulting in very similar conclusions:

> Among the Wanika, a man's blood-money is four slaves or twelve milch cows, a woman's three slaves or nine milch cows. Sick benefit in the English National Insurance Act is 10s a week for men, 7s 6d for women.[66]

(If Parsons' examples now seem somewhat remote to us, no doubt contemporary instances of the principle she illustrates still spring readily enough to mind.) But Parsons' interest in cultural analogies extends well beyond her feminist concerns. In *The Journal of a Feminist* the footnotes of 'E.C.P.' and the observations of Cynthia often draw upon analogies to highlight the nonrational or irrational bases of twentieth-century European-American cultural attitudes. Thus, when Cynthia's socially conservative husband Amos remarks that if a young man visits a

[64] See Hare p. 162.

[65] See Zumwalt p. 233. Lois Palken Rudnick has an account of the fight against the Bursum Bill in her biography of Mabel Dodge Luhan. See *Mabel Dodge Luhan: New Woman, New Worlds*, Albuquerque, New Mexico: University of New Mexico Press, 1984. See also Zumwalt pp. 257–267.

[66] *Old-Fashioned Woman*, p. 201.

prostitute, even without the knowledge of his mother and sister, he 'soils them' by bringing 'a bit of dirtiness into the house', Cynthia reflects that this view of Amos' offers 'a fine modern illustration of the theory of contagious magic'.[67] Similarly, when an acquaintance of Cynthia's who thinks she wants to join a group of men on a hunting trip explains apologetically that 'men sometimes go on such trips, just to get away from women', 'E.C.P.' draws an analogy with the taboos of various African tribes in which contact between women and hunted game is carefully avoided. When young women in the US put on stockings at the onset of puberty, they are practising a ritual covering of nakedness shared with many so-called 'primitive cultures'[68] – and so on. The effect of such analogies is certainly to demonstrate the nonrational bases of many repressive, exclusive or restrictive attitudes to feminine sexuality; but also to call into question the very notion of 'primitiveness'. If members of so-called 'civilized' societies are subject to the same nonrational (and indeed anti-rational) impulses as supposedly 'primitive' peoples, then clearly no such distinction between civilized and primitive can be made. In an essay written during the First World War Parsons makes the point explicitly. 'The spread of ethnological knowledge' would, she hoped, eventually 'undermine the theory of lowly cultural beginnings' and 'even shock certain convictions about the differentiation of cultural groups into lower and higher'.[69] The implications for social progress of a better understanding, based on anthropological data, of the nonrational and antirational foundations of social attitudes are, as Parsons clearly grasps, profound – for the women's movement as for numerous other progressive causes. Parsons derives hope from a belief that the irrational fear of difference and of change that so often proves an obstacle to cultural liberation is fading out of the world:

[67] *The Journal*, p. 16.
[68] *The Journal*, p. 7.
[69] 'The Teleological Delusion', p. 464.

Fear of the unlike and intolerance are due to fear of change, and that fear, whether of change wrought by life or of change threatened by the stranger, that great fear is passing. With it are bound to go the devices of self-protection it prompted – ceremonial, conventionality, and segregation. In this general movement of the human spirit feminism was born; upon its march the hopes of feminism ultimately depend.[70]

Although Parsons subscribes to the notion of a human nature that in certain respects, at least, has altered 'little if at all' over time and in different cultures[71] she does believe, perhaps too optimistically, in a cultural movement towards the acceptance of change and diversity.

It was her readiness to question existing cultural forms, rather than the strictly limited radicalism of her political allegiances, which made Parsons, in William O'Neill's phrase, 'the Left's favorite anthropologist'.[72] One of the first instructors at the ideologically liberal New School for Social Research when it opened in New York in 1919, Parsons was, politically speaking, a liberal social democrat. A year before her death in 1941 she publicly announced her intention to vote for Socialist candidate Norman Thomas in the coming presidential election. The reason she gave – that he was the only candidate 'who seems to understand that...learning to get on with people you disagree with or dislike makes for progress' – suggests not only a certain naiveté about the nature of the fascist regimes the new administration would be required to deal with, but also the definite limits to Parsons' own radical commitment.[73] However, even this degree of mildly left-wing affiliation lends to some of her feminist writing a degree of awareness

---

[70] 'The Teleological Delusion', pp. 463–68.

[71] 'Feminism and Conventionality', *Women in Public Life, Annals of the American Academy of Political and Social Science* 56 (1914): pp. 47–53.

[72] *Fear and Conventionality*, p. xi.

[73] See William L. O'Neill, *Echoes of Revolt: 'The Masses', 1911–1917*, Chicago: Quadrangle, 1966: p. 206.

of working-class women's concerns which the writing of later US feminists was signally to lack. In *The Old-Fashioned Woman*, for instance, she writes of the comparative rates at which the prostitute and the shop worker are compelled to sell their labour power – the prostitute can make seven times the weekly earnings of a department store employee – in terms which at least suggest concern with the economic problems ordinary working women face.[74] As suggested by some of Cynthia's observations in *The Journal of a Feminist* on a feminist meeting of working-class women, Parsons is also aware of contexts in which the interests of upper-class and working-class women come into conflict.[75] Her liberal critique of capitalism is, however, mainly based on a perception that a society based on a principle of individualistic competition disadvantages working mothers of all social classes.[76]

Parsons' vote in 1940 for Norman Thomas was also a vote for his pacifist views. Her own pacifism had its roots in her steadfast intellectual opposition to US intervention in the First World War. Amid the patriotic fervour of the time Parsons continued to declare herself 'non-patriotic'.[77] As with her analyses of patriarchal attitudes and sexism, her examination of the motives behind the jingoistic fervour of the war period discounts contemporary rationalizations to examine the irrational satisfactions militarism offers its collective participants. For the bored male citizens of industrial societies the opportunity for a communal 'bust' or binge in the form of participation in war is, Parsons concludes, highly attractive. In what must be her most scornful dismissal of 'old-fashioned women' unredeemed by feminism, she dismisses such women as too 'scatter-brained and volatile', too unaccustomed to 'steady, protracted effort' to feel any need of breaking out of routine like the men. (Clearly, as a wealthy, leisured

[74] See 'How they Are Voting', *New Republic*, 21 Oct. 1940: p. 554.

[75] *Old-Fashioned Woman*, pp. 197–99.

[76] *The Journal*, pp. 82–83.

[77] 'Do You Believe in Patriotism?' *The Masses*, March 1916: p. 12.

intellectual, Parsons had no direct experience of the routine drudgery of running a household day after day – an occupation involving steady, protracted effort if ever there was one!) More credibly, though, she points out that men, as combatants in warfare, have the consolation of 'gregarious support in their suffering' which women, as non-combatants, by and large do not: 'It is because the hardships of war and even the horrors are suffered together that they are tolerable – and from the same point of view for non-combatants more intolerable.'[78] Thus the male bonding which takes place for men in combat gives them an incentive to engage in warfare which for women, on the whole, does not exist. The will to power also plays a role in making war popular, Parsons contends, – an irrational motive perhaps more likely than others to disguise itself behind intellectual rationalizations. These rationalizations have both social Darwinism and America's Puritan past to draw upon:

> You had only to consider yourself the fittest, for example, to argue that you were the proper survivor, and then did you not cooperate with the will of nature by suppressing the unfit, just as you had cooperated with the will of God by suppressing the wicked or the impious?[79]

As elsewhere in her writing Parsons also employs anthropological analogies to develop an understanding of the strategies by which public acceptance of the US intervention is secured. Rituals of 'ceremonial impatience' are used by citizens to hasten the war's end. The giant thermometers on the wartime village greens, marked to indicate the numbers of war bonds sold, are 'expressive paraphernalia' of these rituals. In her essay 'Patterns for

---

[78] 'On the Loose', *New Republic*, 27 Feb. 1915: pp. 100–101. Parsons considered that Randolph Bourne, a fellow-pacifist whom she admired and respected, underestimated this irrational emotional investment of the average citizen in the ruling-class 'sport' of war. See her 'A Pacifist Patriot', a review of Bourne's *Untimely Papers*, published in *The Dial*, March 1920, pp. 367–70.

[79] 'The Teleological Delusion', p. 464.

Peace or War', published in September 1917, Parsons examines the process of acculturation whereby, for example, a Pueblo community assimilates a Catholic festival to its original sacred ritual of the Day of the Dead. She goes on to argue that a similar, but in this case politically motivated, process of acculturation is at work in the US government's evocation of past American history to justify US entry into the First World War: 'Once the European War was classified as a war for liberty with the war of American Independence or the Civil War, the European war was acculturated.'[80]

Whatever the truth of Parsons' observations on the psychological factors involved in support for militarism, in another context she does offer an astute analysis of the economic motives behind the US intervention in the war. So long, she points out, as the intervention can be justified as a source of war profits for US capitalists, it will enjoy their support. If, however, taxation imposed on US business for the sake of the war effort becomes burdensome, the American businessman will become a pacifist overnight. In short, 'The effect of war upon business is the touchstone in this country for the desirability of war'. Parsons presciently foresaw the future usefulness to the 'plutocracy', as she calls the bourgeoisie of North America, of a series of 'little wars' which while ostensibly 'for the good of 'backward peoples' would benefit US commerce and finance. 'Thus for the good of others,' she wrote, 'we may become a militarist people without knowing it until some day...we find ourselves with a fight against the rest of the world on our hands.'[81]

The great strength of Parsons' social analyses, though, remains their shrewd psychology. Her thought on a range of social issues is informed by close scrutiny of the irrational motives underlying the rationalizations of conservative and conformist thinkers, and by an awareness of the will to power which lurks behind so many human

---

[80] 'Patterns for Peace or War', *Scientific Monthly*, Sept. 1917: pp. 229–38.

[81] 'Patterns for Peace or War', p. 238.

pretensions to idealism. Her own declared interest in
conducting such analyses is the promotion of individuality
and diversity. Where this last point is concerned, Parsons
suggests convincingly that the supposed 'tolerance' of US
society is actually a function of an anti-intellectual
'indifference to opinion'. The intellectual innovator who
forgets his or her place on the margins of society 'may
count on quick suppression'. For all such innovators, 'the
price of existence is remaining ornamental'.[82] One element
of Parsons' own effectiveness as a subversive thinker
undoubtedly lies in her ability to seem merely 'ornamental',
a scholarly writer on arcane intellectual topics of little
obvious concern to the ordinary citizen. The reader who
attends carefully to the subtleties of her understated,
elliptical, ironic prose, is apt to be surprised, even shocked
by the radicalism of ideas so quietly voiced. Cynthia, in
The Journal of a Feminist, is rather more outspoken than
her creator, but equally ironic in her social vision, and
equally bent on subverting various aspects of the *status
quo*. She, like Parsons, is a sharp detector of hypocrisy and
intellectual confusion, a champion of the individual against
the tyrannies of outworn convention and of those who
invoke such convention to bolster their own self-esteem.
She too wishes for every woman – and every man – to live
'a life aglow through their imagination' – a 'free and
passionate life'.[83]

'Her death is a loss to the nation', wrote Parsons' friend,
mentor and fellow-anthropologist Franz Boas when
Parsons died in 1941.[84] For those feminists and critics of
the *status quo* who care to examine it, her legacy remains.

[82] 'Patterns for Peace or War', p. 238.

[83] *The Journal*, p. 47.

[84] 'Elsie Clews Parsons', p. 90.

The Journal of a Feminist offers a convenient introduction to Parsons' ideas. Her other works, although mostly out of print, are available in university libraries in Britain and the United States. (*The Old-Fashioned Woman* was reprinted by the Arno Press in 1972; *Pueblo Indian Religion* by Midway Reprints, University of Chicago Press, in 1974; and *Religious Chastity* by the AMS Press, in 1975.)

There are now two full-length studies of Elsie Clews Parsons' life and work. *A Woman's Quest for Science* (1985), by Parsons' great-nephew Peter Hare, draws extensively on private papers and family records for its biographical detail. *Wealth and Rebellion* (1992), by anthropologist Rosemary Levy Zumvalt, builds on the Hare biography, but also offers new biographical insights, and a thorough and fascinating account of Parsons' professional work in anthropology. There are brief tributes and biographical notes by Randolph Bourne (1917), Clarence Day (1919), Franz Boas (1942), and Alfred Louis Kroeber (1943). (See Bibliography.) *Notable American Women* (1980) contains a necessarily short, but useful, biographical entry. My *Heretics and Hellraisers* (1993) considers Parsons' early social criticism in the context of her association with the radical intellectuals of Greenwich Village. William L. O'Neill's study of *The Masses*, *Echoes of Revolt* (1966) and Judith Schwartz's *Radical Feminists of Heterodoxy* (1982) also briefly deal with Parsons in this Greenwich Village context. Eric Sandeen's article 'Bourne Again' (1989) discusses Randolph Bourne's correspondence with Parsons (although the article's emphasis is mainly on Bourne). Margaret Sanger's *Autobiography* (1938) makes passing mention of Parsons' support for Sanger during the latter's prosecution for teaching about birth control. Lois Palken Rudnick's biography of Mabel Dodge Luhan, *New Woman, New Worlds* (1984) alludes to Parsons' involvement in the fight against the Bursum Bill. A few pages in Margaret M. Caffrey's *Ruth Benedict: Stranger in this Land* (1989) deal with Parsons as a teacher and benefactor of the younger anthropologist.

The Elsie Clews Parsons Papers, including the original manuscript of *The Journal of a Feminist*, are in the keeping of the American Philosophical Society in Philadelphia. Further material is held in the Oral History Collection of Columbia University, New York.

Margaret C. Jones
Bristol, 1994

Elsie and Lissa, 1902 (courtesy of Fanny Parsons Culleton)

Elsie in her riding habit, ready for fieldwork,
circa 1915 (courtesy of Fanny Parsons Culleton)

A NOTE ON THE TEXT

In editing Elsie Parsons' original text I have occasionally standardized punctuation (for example altering '–' to the more usual '...' throughout). I have retained American spelling except where Parsons herself uses a 'British' form – as in her spelling with a 'u' of words like 'colour' and 'favour'. Where Parsons in revising her original manuscript of *The Journal of a Feminist* has made significant cuts, I have indicated these by placing phrases and sentences removed in the revised version in square brackets [ ].

Notes designated by Arabic numerals refer to the Editor's Introduction, and to my notes to Parsons' text. Alphabetical references are used to indicate the footnotes of 'E.C.P.' to Cynthia's *Journal*. The occasional asterisk – * – indicates a note appended by Cynthia herself.

All page numbers given for *The Journal of a Feminist* in the Editor's Notes refer to the present published version of *The Journal*.

PARSONS' INTRODUCTION TO
THE JOURNAL OF A FEMINIST

'The least you can do,' I am told by the keeper of this diary, 'is to write an introduction. It was you who bade me write it, and you are really responsible for the opinion that it is worth the publishing. Besides you must show up in some way those ethnographic parallels[1] you talk about so much. You told me, you remember, a journal of this kind would be a contribution to ethnogaphy. It is up to you to say so openly.'

I will. The parallels let me try to draw in footnotes. As to the general ethnographic quality or purport of the journal a word or two here. As a record of social practices or habits the journal is not unlike that kept by any observer of society whether on the West Coast of Africa or in the drawing-rooms of London or New York; but as a record of the differences in mentality met in the same society it makes a picture that the sojourner among savages rarely if ever undertakes at all and that the drawing-room portraitist, the novelist, usually colours up to match tradition or tones in other ways to please his reader. Of these differences in mentality Professor Lévy-Bruhl[2] gave us a few years ago an

---

[1] 'ethnographic parallels...'. Parsons alludes to her method of drawing analogies between the beliefs and practices of so-called 'primitive' and so-called 'civilized' cultures. For a more detailed discussion of this technique, see Editor's Introduction, above.

[2] Lucien Lévy-Bruhl (1857-1939), sociologist and ethnologist. Parsons refers to Lévy-Bruhl's *Les fonctions mentales dans les sociétés inférieures* (1910), translated in 1926 as *How Natives Think* (New York: Washington Square Press, 1966). In *Les fonctions mentales* Lévy-Bruhl does not hesitate to write of 'primitive cultures.' It is to Parsons' credit that she came to criticize (as, much later, did Levy-Bruhl himself)

enlightening analysis. Primitive mind, he affirms, deals mostly with mystical, prelogical representations; the logical concepts develop later. The representation has an aura of emotions and of impulses from which the concept is free. The representation is prelogical because contradictions in fact do not concern it; and it is mystical dealing as it does with the subjective aspect of things regardless of objective reality. Prone to this mystical attitude a man does not dissociate himself from his representations. He is part of them, and let me add he is most at peace when his associations are least disturbed. Out of this sense of participation many group practices and customs arise. Such instances of the 'law of participation' are more characteristic of savage society than of civilized, but there is much in civilization which is based on them – they are at the bottom of our institutional life. Collective representations play the major part too in social intercourse; they may never be ignored in discussion, much less in social reform, if only, as Thomas Wentworth Higginson[3] points out in his charming reference to the sacred obscurity of the Invisible Lady, because 'every reformer needs to fortify his position by showing examples of the original attitude from which society has been gradually emerging'.[a] Mr. Higginson and every other

---

[a] *Women and the Alphabet*, p.71, Boston and New York, 1990

the racist habits of thought with which Parsons' initial training in ethnology were so deeply imbued.

Lévy-Bruhl argued that 'collective representations' may be recognized by certain signs: 'They are common to the members of a given social group' and 'they are transmitted from one generation to another.' Above all, they awaken in individuals possessed by them fundamentally irrational and unquestioning 'sentiments of respect, fear, adoration, and so on...' (*How Natives Think*, 3).

Whereas Lévy-Bruhl at the time of writing *Les fonctions mentales* believed that 'the mental processes' of 'primitives' did not 'coincide with those which we are accustomed to describe in men of our own type', Parsons constantly implies that so-called 'primitives' and so-called 'civilized peoples' share in common a far greater degree of irrationality than the members of supposedly 'civilized' cultures generally cared to admit.

[3] Thomas Wentworth Higginson (1823–1911), activist for the abolition of slavery. Served as colonel of the first black regiment in the Union army during the US Civil War. Campaigned for women's rights – notably for suffrage.

feminist is much too rationalistic not to be baffled again and again by the representations of anti-feminism. But the merely observant ethnologist is also baffled by them. Labeling them 'primitive', classifying them as illustrations of sympathetic magic, of magic contagious or homeopathic, of the law of participation or of a logic unconcerned by contradictions does not really get him very far.[b] Closer observation is what he needs. There are practices and points of view today which once they have passed out of the region of collective representation unobserved in detail will be as obscure to our descendants as the couvade, let us say, is to us, or rites of veiling or rules of exogamy or teknonymy or avoidance practices. Even today it is difficult for us to comprehend the attitude of the past generation on many matters, on age-classes, on caste, on religion, on sex.

Towards sex their attitude is particularly baffling, just as ours is bound to be, it is easy to realize, to those who come after. Hence it occurred to me that a record of our tangle of feelings and ideas about sex, about such questions of sex as are encountered day by day, might make a pattern of some value for those to come, a pattern not by any means lessening their surprise over the intricacy of it all, but leaving certain subjects and their connections, perhaps at points not easily now foreseen, less obscure and bewildering.

Here was my reason for suggesting the keeping of a journal to a friend whose experiences, I knew, were broad enough and commonplace enough to make her record typical. As to her power of observation and her facility of expression I leave the reader to judge. Having known her for a long time and under varied and trying circumstances I am willing, however, to vouch for her sincerity and truthfulness. Changes in personal nouns, changes quite insignificant for the reader, she has made no doubt, and in certain instances she has altered, she tells me, those circumstances in tale or anecdote which might betray a

[b] Nevertheless for the most striking of such illustrations in this journal see pp. [unfinished ref.].

confidence. But such circumstances are also as a rule
without significance for the reader. More notable than her
alterations are her omissions. What she has written is but a
small part of what a journal kept by her without reserves or
restrictions would record – topics too personal, as we say,
for publication, or for that matter for writing up of any
kind or topics devoid of any feminist bearing or interest.
Her life is not meagre or barren, nor is she as obsessed as
most feminists, particularly feminists of the strictly
suffragist variety, by the feminist movement; her other
interests are vital and far-reaching. A feminist bias she has
of course, but this bias I do not regret, nor should the
reader, for it is a part of the very pattern she is drawing.
And my caution to her while indulging in commentary to
avoid propaganda she has on the whole heeded – probably
with considerable self-restraint. For she is naturally a
reformer, not merely an iconoclast, and to most of us she
does appear to take her sex – but fortunately not herself – a
little seriously. As to her opinions obviously I am not
called upon either to agree or to disagree and for them I
assume of course no more responsibility than if they were
the expressions of a Hottentot or a South Sea Islander.
They interest me primarily, I must confess, because they are
representative, howbeit of a comparatively small class. For
this degree of detachment she will forgive me, I trust.

  She may forgive me also if I conclude with a biographical
note,[4] a word or two merely to complete her own pattern,
to give by 'placing' her the proper angle to her picture. Of
Anglo-Saxon parents, her father of the English middle-
class, an immigrant to this country as a youth, her mother a
'well-born' Southerner, she was brought up in one of the
plutocratic circles of New York in the eighties and nineties.
In this closed circle, 'Pley thou not but with thy peres' was
a refrain, a more incessant refrain, I suspect, than ever it
could have been in a feudal century. Nevertheless, from
childhood the girl was by the way of making friends on the

---

[4] This biographical note corresponds closely to Parsons' own life history.
See Editor's Introduction, above.

outside – at first in the city parks where the children of the rich were less closely shepherded then than now – later, when she became truly rebellious, in the social settlements and among the social reformers of the town; and she went to college, quite an adventure in those days for a New York girl of her class.

She is the mother of children enough to entitle – or condemn – her to be called old-fashioned.[5] She writes a little for the magazines, and she has published one novel. She is interested in public affairs and in public opinion. She has been a student, she tells me, from the time 'London Bridge' became one of her favorite games because it was so interesting to see how 'My Fair Lady' would make her choice – between pink and blue, between apple and pear, the latter at least a more important decision than may at first sight appear, Lavengro notwithstanding.[6]

Now I have stated, I think, all that is necessary to know in advance about the journalist. Perhaps I should add that she has been of late years in many of the out-of-the-way parts of America – parts utterly foreign to the oblivious New Yorker, but that her last journey to the Old World was made eleven years ago.

---

[5] *The Old-Fashioned Woman* is both the title of one of Parsons' most explicitly feminist works, and a pervasive term in her writings to describe a woman exclusively preoccupied with domesticity and motherhood. Later in *The Journal* Cynthia portrays a typical example of such 'old-fashioned' attitudes p. 81.

[6] Lavengro. Rather an obscure allusion, apparently to George Borrow's novel *Lavengro* (1851).

THE JOURNAL OF A FEMINIST

Newport.

I begin with yesterday – August 15, 1913 – for it was yesterday came the letter which put the idea of keeping a journal into my head. Besides the conversation we had yesterday after lunch at Katherine's makes as proper a beginning as another.

The place is the island in Naragansett Bay a Dutch navigator put down on his chart as the Red Island, the Dutch perhaps for the *couleur du rose* in which he and many since have seen it. To be sure some of its rocks are red or pink. But then they are also blue or amber or purple or orange.

The scene is a grassy terrace with privet hedges and blooming rose bushes and marble balustrade on either hand, behind us the French windows of a summer palace, in front cliffs and a blue sea beyond.

The persons – our hostess asleep most of the time on the inviting turf, Dr Herbert Walters, an eminent New York surgeon, F—, a popular magazine editor, and Frank Ascot, a diverting writer on the passing show. Frank talks even better than he writes, and as a promoter of the pastime known as general conversation he is unequalled. Yesterday as we sat there smoking, all rather lazy after our morning swim, he decided to set the ball rolling with: 'Cynthia tells me she has no sense of modesty about clothes.' 'Perhaps I haven't,' I spoke up, 'but of course what I did say to you yesterday was that women had far less of that kind of modesty than men.' 'Didn't you say you always undressed with the blinds up?' 'Yes, I do.' 'Why do you?' asked F—, obviously curious. 'Because I like the sun and air and don't feel responsible for the taste or morals of people who spy.' 'Would you disrobe for us here at this moment?' asked F—

again, unabashed. 'No, I wouldn't.' 'Why not?' He *was* persistent. 'Can't you see the difference between undressing in your room unconcerned about the passerby and gratifying what *might* be – I tried to soften it – just might be a vulgar curiosity?' 'Well, some women *do* make a display of themselves to arouse it', put in Frank the pacificator. 'Of course they do – what do these slit skirts and diaphanous affairs mean but just that?' asseverated F— 'They are far more conventional than you think,' spoke up Dr Walters, taking as usual the right moment to carry conviction. 'Woman's modesty or immodesty finds expression much less in her dress than men generally think. Much of woman's so-called modesty is nothing but a man's armor at any rate.' 'Yes, a kind of vicarious shield', concluded our hostess, waking up. 'I've been dreaming about that poor forlorn man Maurice Hewlitt writes about. He undertook to domesticate a fairy and he tried to make her modest by stalking off whenever she let her cobweb dress slip off her little shoulders...' 'Do you think F— [Boyden] got your point, Herbert?' I asked as he and I were motoring back to the house where we are both staying. 'He got my point, all right. Of course a man like that, a fine, vigorous brute, is all the time battling against his natural instincts and he grabs at every convention and tradition for help. But he got my point.'

I may have given others besides Frank Ascot [Hal Rhodes] reason since I've been here to question my sense of modesty in clothes. In swimming I wear no stockings – except weekends when Amos goes down to the beach with me.[7] 'Do you care?' I asked him to make quite sure. 'Yes, I think you'd better wear them', he answered.... At other times I'm the only female on the beach not to wear them, or rather the only female over fourteen.[c] It's rather curious how the bestockinged take it. Everyone says, 'That's just what I'd like to do'. Of course one can't resist rejoining,

[c] Wearing stockings in bathing seems to be part of our ritual for adolescence, just as in many savage tribes girls put on clothes for the first time at that period *E.C.P.*

[7] Amos is Cynthia's conservative-minded spouse, closely modelled on Elsie Parsons' husband Herbert.

'Why don't you?' The answer, I have discovered, falls into one of two formulas. It is 'Because my legs are not as good looking as yours' (with less gracious or more downright variations), or it is, 'Because I'd not be let'. I make bets with myself now which formula I am to get. It's a kind of *London Bridge.* 'I'd not be let,' or 'I'd not let myself.' One doesn't always predict right. But I do predict with certainty that no woman will ever tell me she thinks stockingless legs indecorous. I would like to make that assertion to F— sometime – just to hear him say: 'Ah, but you don't know what the men on Coddington's Beach think.'

Newport, August 16.
What one of them at least must think is quite evident from what happened there, I am told, today. Someone went in wearing 'maillots', the skirtless, stockingless bathing suit European women wear, and before she left the beach someone was requested by the President of the Coddington's Beach Association not to wear it again.[8] It was my skirt that saved me…. When I told this incident to a friend who sailed over this afternoon from the less sophisticated mainland he said it prompted him to relate a story of one of its remoter beaches. 'I had walked across country to it for a swim, but just as I was about to take off my clothes, the only figure on it I thought, along came a couple, a man and a woman, both well on in middle age, plain people, New England natives. The woman walked on, but the man stopped to exchange the time of day and ask a question or two about the locality. I was there for a swim I told him.

Perhaps he and his wife would walk on a way, if she minded. 'Oh, we don't mind,' he said, 'we often take one ourselves in our tramps.' And verily as I was dressing after my swim, didn't I see them going in together at the end of the beach as simply and unselfconsciously as a pair of children. 'More so, I fancy, for few are so conservative

---

[8] 'Someone went in…' It was actually Parsons herself who committed this grave offence on the socially exclusive Bailey's Beach (here named Coddington's Beach) in Newport, Rhode Island. See Zumwalt pp. 28–29.

about clothes as children, except savages[d] and the President of Coddington's Beach Association.... It's plain why you told me your anecdote. How vulgar it makes us seem on our fashionable beach.'

August 17.
We are vulgar indeed! There is a Russian here in love, they say, with pretty Mrs S. Whenever you see her you may be sure within half a minute – he being a European – to see him. Being a European he is reticent, but not secretive, a point of view not only not held by the native American but not always respected. It was not by one of them the other night. He happened to be motoring behind Mrs S's motor, he said, and his searchlight *happened*, he *said*, to turn on the motor ahead at a moment when its occupants did not foresee a searchlight. And now all Newport, fashionable Newport, is talking about that flashlight picture as they call it.... I sat next to the Russian the other night at dinner. He told me the story of a little adventure he had had the night before at a dance. 'I was standing on the terrace smoking a cigarette. There was a light not far away in the garden and silhouetted against it were a girl I knew and liked and a man. They were talking quite earnestly together. Presently I see a man jump out from behind one bush and run over to the bush near that couple and drop down on the ground. I run to the bush too and I kick him twice in the head before he goes off...one of your reporters.... And it was a girl I liked.'
I told that story to the woman who told me the searchlight 'joke'. 'Good for him!' she cried, 'I like him for it. It's because he's a Russian that he did it. That's the way to treat those dirty reporters.' But it isn't 'those dirty

[d] Savages may be extremely meticulous about undressing. 'The men carry their physical modesty further than do Europeans,' writes Seligmann of a New Guinea tribe, 'for no one takes off his perineal bandage when bathing, and a native would be almost as much ashamed to remove this before a single kinsman as he would be to stalk naked through his hamlet. Women are equally particular and are said never to strip before one another.' (*The Melanesians of New Guinea*, p. 568.) E.C.P.

reporters' who are joking – as yet – about the flashlight picture, and Russian gallantry is hardly finding its reward.

Newport, August 19.
I had another talk *á la Russe* with a secretary of embassy last night. It was at a dance, on the verandah. He had asked me to lend him a book I had been citing. 'No, I'm not going to.' 'Why?' And knowing that he very well knew why I answered: 'I just couldn't.' 'No reason.' 'The best; I gave it only today to a more important request.' 'Why did he ask?' 'Because he was an American. American men always ask if they may.' 'Then they are – asses.' 'Of course they're asses – but nice asses. And perhaps in the long run more successful than you Europeans', a retort we both knew was pure bluff, justifiable in a countrywoman, he may have thought, for he let it pass with a shrug, and as one of the 'nice asses' asked me at that moment to dance our colloquy fitly terminated.

He *was* a nice ass and he revealed it to me unexpectedly. 'I've read your novel', he said when we sat down. 'And I'd like to know – if you don't mind telling me' – I'd seen it coming in his first sentence, he was an unsophisticated New York business man, a 'family man' – 'I'd like to know if you think it's decent for a man no longer in love with his wife, to fall in love with someone else. He's fond of his wife, you know.' So, that was it... I knew his wifely little wife.... It was a responsibility. He added uncertainly: 'Most husbands aren't faithful, you know.' Poor man, he was in the trap of the old bullying catch-words. 'Of course if the wife is the sort of woman who can't bear knowing, he will be considerate of her? She mustn't know.' 'Yes, of course.' 'And he will give both women the best of himself, the best each will take?' That needed amplification – for him, but here we were interrupted. It was an overambitious conversation for a dance, at any rate.

Newport, August 20.
I had another something like it – but with a difference – today, canoeing. This husband had already experimented,

it was said, and disastrously. He was an older man, and an artist; but his initial question was almost identical. He got the same answer. 'But supposing the wife, she's not in love with her husband either, remember, still thinks it an indignity?' How the deuce did he expect me to answer. It was *his* wife. 'There are monopolies one can't recognize,' I said. 'Shall we paddle over to those rocks?' The rockweed has a marvellous glisten in this sunset light. They *do* consult me as a sort of mother confessor. I'm supposed to have 'views', you see, on almost any question between the sexes, having written a story about some of them – such is the magic of the printed word....

It isn't only the men who drive me into the corner of their own perplexity. My hostess here has a younger brother, much younger. She is of my mother's generation, he of mine. This brother is to marry a certain charming lady – when she gets her divorce. It's a situation very trying to my hostess and from time to time she unburdens herself to me. 'It won't last', is her refrain. That the lady in question is as charming as a lady can be, she concedes, that she is as much entitled to a divorce as ever a lady was, she concedes, that her brother is very much in love with her and she with him, she concedes, but she has framed in the affair for herself with, 'I wouldn't mind so much if I thought it would last', and from the set of that phrase there seems to be no escape. 'It won't last' – but neither does the spring, nor a baby, nor the taste of a nectarine, I remark to her unlistening ears. 'Why must you banish bliss because it's fleeting or forego a pleasure or a joy because it's shortlived?... Our ideas do connect up in such odd ways. Because the shortlived is in its ending upsetting or painful we tag it as trivial or worthless or immoral. It's a way we have of insisting to ourselves that good things are permanent. If they're not permanent, we say, they are not good, or if we must have them good and are quite unable to blink the fact of their transiency we say they are links in a chain of cause and effect. Evolutionary theory is no end of a comfort to the moralist.' But it wasn't for the time being to my hostess. 'I give them just two years together,'

she lamented, 'one for happiness, one for unhappiness.'
'Not such an unusual proportion, if you must make one in
terms of time', I said.

August 22.
It *is* the attribute of permanence which seems to justify
marriage in the mind of those to whom any other sex
relation is unjustifiable. Why? Should not any relation
between two persons be judged – if judged at all – for what
it is at the time being, not for what it has been or even may
be? Clinging to a relationship of the past, a moribund or
dead relationship, will be recognized as a sin some day, one
of those still unnamed, innumerable sins the triumph of
personal morality over status morality will bring in its
train. Now, however, in marriage at least this adhesion to
what exists no longer is commonly praised, stamped an act
of self-sacrifice, and so according to our Eastern faith
indisputably right – nature notwithstanding. Three of the
victims of such a refusal to recognize the present I meet
here from day to day, the mask of their unhappiness too
flimsy to disguise. To the plaudits of all, she has assumed
the role of the faithful wife – whether from vanity or
affection or inertia I know her too little to guess. 'How
long will it take her, I wonder, to find out that she is
making three persons wretched for – a theory that is
passing?' I asked my hostess. 'Surely you don't believe in
'free love'!' and in the horror her words expressed the kind
lady betrayed her nearness to the generation that was
bullied out of comfortable clothes and of the franchise by
that bludgeon of a phrase. 'I believe that love should be
free', I answered soothingly if tritely. Besides the only
answer to a catchword is another.

August 23. 'The catchwords of morality are endless', said
Herbert today, as I depicted to him the dismay of our
hostess over my 'loose' ideas. So are its masks. Your
Faithful Wife, I suspect, is wearing one of them.... There
are women who make a virtue of not going the entire way
of love just as there are men who take credit to themselves

for not being drunkards – from sheer self-delusion. In both cases they stop short because the phase of excitement, of enjoyment, of exaltation is followed by a phase of purely physiological inhibition. It would actually be painful to them to traverse it, but upon not traversing it they plume themselves.' 'And seem,' I concluded, 'that is, if they are American women, 'as good as gold,' to use the expression a baffled European once used to me about them...'. It was an expression of respect, but the Englishman who used it didn't think of us or at least of that trait in us with respect. Like others he was merely playing into the hands of the enemy by using their phraseology. He happened to be nothing but a pirate, but propagandists do no better for themselves. When feminists talk of seduction, adultery, violation, they lay their hands on the table before they begin the game, the match of free relations against proprietary.

Lenox, August 24.
I was ahead of time in the Newport station today to take the train to Lenox,[9] so I walked along the platform and smoked a cigarette. When I travel alone I am apt to smoke in railway stations – because I feel like smoking and there's no place on the train to smoke. Incidentally it's of some benefit too to the public. As soon as I begin to smoke in a railway station – or any other public place – I become the object of concentrated attention, on the part of the more polite of a solemn or frankly amused attention, on the part of the class less pretentious of civility, of the track laborers, for examaple, of a kind of leering attention, a notice which passes sometimes into jeers. The way a man takes a woman's smoking is today almost an unfailing mark of class – if one wishes to keep to the time-honored classification of the lower, the middle and the upper. The middle class man is surprised by it, disconcerted or disapproving, or perhaps merely amused – it is funny or it is disgusting; of the attitude of the other two classes I had illustrations

[9] The Parsons family owned a farm in Lenox, Massachusetts, where Parsons did much of her writing.

today on the Newport platform. Two railway hands were sitting idle a little way off. 'Give us a light', called out one – into space, and both grinned and guffawed as unselfconsciously as the lookers-on at the sort of indecent play the New York Police Department has no prejudice against.... Presently a young man in whose mother's house I had recently dined joined me on the platform. In a moment or two he took out his cigarette case and, being without a match, he lit his cigarette from mine....

Last winter in my train north from Mexico City there was as we started but one other passenger in my car, a French shop keeper, a smoker, I noticed. After breakfast I returned to my seat and lit a cigarette. Up steps the conductor, an American *del Norte*. 'Perhaps you do not know, lady, it's against the rule for ladies to smoke on the train in the United States.' 'But we're not in the United States.' 'No, but this is an American Pullman car.' 'Do you provide a smoking car for ladies?' 'No.' 'Where do you expect me to smoke then?' 'You might go into the ladies' dressing-room.' 'Rather stuffy in there, isn't it?' 'Well, I tell you what you can do, when I'm not looking, go into the end compartment of this car. It's empty. It's against the rule of the company for conductors to smoke too, but I sometimes go in there myself. I know what it's like to want a smoke.' The friendly soul! And it *was* decent of him to take me on as a fellow criminal.... On Mexican cars it isn't against the rule for either conductors or 'ladies' to smoke.

Today out of Boston as I was cutting out a story from a newspaper, I caught the eye of my vis-à-vis, a plainly dressed, stout, middle-aged and rather alert-eyed woman. She was from the Pacific coast, she told me later, and remarking on my Phi Beta Kappa key, a college graduate. 'What do you think of that?' I asked, handing her the newspaper cutting to read. It read: 'The undersigned regrets to state that his wife, —, had, without reasonable cause, quitted his bed and board, and that therefore he will not after this time be responsible for any debts contracted by her...'. There had never been any indication, the article went on to say, that Mr and Mrs — were not living happily together. They were married in 1886. 'Well?' I queried as she came to the end of it. 'And they've been married such a long time too.' College graduate or not, it is the personal relation that interests, and the idea that no situation endured long enough can become unendurable that prevails. 'But what do you think of the method he takes, and the language?' 'He may have been driven to it of course, you can't tell.... Still the wording is of course humiliating – even if it is a mere legal form. Why *don't* men give up using such expressions?' 'Would you if you were a woman lawyer?' 'I don't believe in women being lawyers,' she answered and she gathered up her things and left the train at the next station before I could ask her 'Why?'

September 1.
'How we do move!' I exclaimed this morning to Amos as I took off the wrapping of a copy of *Harper's Weekly*. Staring one in the face on the magazine cover was the caption, 'Unmarried Mothers'. 'And I've just had another instance of our pace', I added. 'Ann (my maid, a young English immigrant) has been asking me to lend her 'Damaged Goods'. A friend of hers had been to see the play.'[10] 'I hope you won't', rejoined Amos. 'That play was a great mistake. Plays like that only arouse pruriency.'
     Later as he and I were driving together over the hills I picked up the subject again. Knowing that he has acquired a considerable interest in eugenics since he has become the executor of an estate which has endowed several eugenic projects, and knowing too that he is a member of the Society for Social and Moral Prophylaxis, his criticism of *Les Avariés* is provocative.... 'You don't think that a play

[10] *Damaged Goods (Les Avariés).* Eugène Brieux's play about sexually transmitted disease is a heavily didactic, not to say moralistic play, which attempts to dispel the fear and repressive silence surrounding the subject. As the play's hero, a doctor, puts it, 'Young men ought to be taught the responsibilities they assume and the misfortunes they may bring on themselves', if they engage in sexual relations in ignorance of sexual hygiene p. 239.

as painful as 'Damaged Goods' stimulates the impulses of sex, do you?' I asked, knowing that any sex stimulant, any readily recognized stimulant I mean of course, was anathema, and so intending to start clear of that particular reef of argument. 'No, but it familiarizes people with the subject of prostitution. That's how it does harm. I think people ought to know about prostitution, but the actualities of it ought to be kept out of sight. A boy ought to be kept from knowing how accessible it is. Once when I was a student in Berlin I went with two fellows into a drinking place on Frederickstrasse where men picked up women. It was one of the most revolting sights I'd ever seen; but I've always been sorry I saw it. I'd have been better off not seeing it.... What helps a boy more than anything else is the sense that the thing is remote from his daily life, foreign, that his mother and sister don't know anything about it, that if he indulges in it he soils them, he brings a bit of dirtiness into the house.' [What a fine modern illustration of the theory of contagious magic, I thought, but I said:] 'You believe though in the mother and sister *knowing*.' 'Yes, but not in their *talking*. I don't want them to go to a play like 'Damaged Goods' and then discuss it at home. The boy mustn't know that they know.... Besides, 'Damaged Goods' only tells the public that the chance of catching syphilis is comparatively slight, too slight to be a deterrent. More than that, that there is a cure for it, and a prophylactic. That sort of knowledge may only increase prostitution.' 'Of course – there're two sides to prostitution, the hygienic and the moral, and we may wipe out venereal disease altogether and still have the moral side.... 'What is the prophylactic?' 'I don't know. They use it in the Navy; they ought to use it in the Army; but what it is I don't know.' 'A drug?' '*I don't know and I don't want to know.*' The desire not to know is puzzling and rather baffling, so I stopped talking and looked about for signs of autumn in the woods our road was crossing – a reddening sumach, wood asters...where the woods thinned to the road. As we neared the lake, Amos checked the horses for the view we liked and then, unprompted, he went on: 'There are legislative ways too of dealing with venereal disease – I believe in compulsory marriage health certificates, in making the communication of venereal disease in marriage a felony, and in disqualifying diseased persons for public positions compelling all public officials and servants to be periodically examined.' 'Rather drastic, that last provision, don't you think, considering venereal disease is an infection acquired in more than one way and that it may not handicap a person in work. But how are you going to arouse the public enough to make the passing of such legislation possible? Isn't a play like 'Damaged Goods' just the thing to create 'public sentiment?' 'It's not necessary. The rightminded kind of a governor could get through such legislation.' 'I happen to know that a bill penalizing the communication of venereal disease in marriage has been pending in the New York State Legislature for quite a while. Two years ago a woman told me that she and her doctor husband had both turned woman suffragists because of their conviction that the New York Legislature would not pass that bill until women had a vote.... Even if you got the laws without public pressure, would they be enforced without public opinion behind them? Wouldn't they merely lead to blackmail and official corruption just like our New York laws to suppress prostitution?' My question was not met, for my comparison was taken advantage of. 'There's only one way to meet prostitution,' Amos went on, 'Boys must be taught to avoid temptation and to practise self-control. 'Lead us not into temptation' should be their constant prayer.' 'Is the teaching to be general or specific?' 'General. Of course I'd have both boys and girls taught at a suitable age the facts of procreation, boys by their fathers, girls by their mothers.... But perhaps at present the teaching will have to be done in the schools. I think a fifteen minute talk would be enough, given with a solemn moral emphasis.' 'You rely on the direction of youth; but prostitution is not an affair merely of youth. It may be for the women involved in it, perhaps, for the life of the prostitute, they say, is short.[e]

[e]   Recent data belie this common statement. See Flexner.... *E.C.P.*

But among their patrons, there's a very large proportion, I'm told, of older men, married men.' 'I question that – outside of the limited circles of the rich.' There we halted the discussion to talk after a more desultory fashion, or, what is even better at times behind horses, not at all.... And so that is Amos' program – more repressive legislation and – a fifteen minutes talk to boys and girls.... It is sometimes proposed to lengthen the talk, and during the next decade new kinds of drastic legislation are sure to be advocated. During this time will the real questions aroused by prostitution be answered or even raised? I doubt it. Prostitution is only one of our devices for driving sex into a corner. Marriage is another; the life of religious chastity, another; the life of art for art's sake another; athletics, another; the discussion of sex problems another, a new corner – and the old game of puss-in-the-corner will go merrily on – or sadly – until we enjoy a change of heart about the value of sex to life.

September 14.
'There's Munsterberg for you!' cried Herbert this morning, waving a piece of the Sunday *Times* at me. 'He's down on sex plays too. He says that any kind of thinking on sex questions stimulates the sex organs and that for a people to try to improve its sexual morality by dragging its problems into the street is a kind of Munchausen performance[11] of lifting themselves up by their scalps.' 'Perhaps my ideas of improving sexual morality are not quite the same as yours and Munsterberg's and I may not be as terrified as you two by the possibility of stimulating the sexual organism. But there are others who are. Here's an account of how a woman's club in San Francisco held an *auto da fé* for Shaw's book of Brieux's plays[12] – they were so 'shocked'.'

[11] Munchausen performance. This seems to be an allusion to Karl Friedrich Hieronymus, Baron von Munchhausen (1720–97) whose name became legendary as that of a teller of tall tales about impossible physical feats.

[12] Shaw's book.... See the edition of Brieux's plays edited with a preface by George Bernard Shaw, with plays translated by 'Mrs Bernard Shaw'. St John Hankin and John Pollock. (London: Fifield, 1911.)

'You'll have to burn some of the books in your library yourself or put them out of sight when John is a few years older.' [John is my eldest son.][13] 'I doubt if I do. John and I are following a different path together. I have not been waiting to have a fifteen minute talk with him. John knew before his younger brothers were born that they were expected. John knows what a woman's body – my body – looks like, and what its parts and the parts of his own body are called. Such a thing as a 'moral talk' we have never had, but if I had any doubt of his knowing my point of view or of his having one of his own, a little incident that occurred a year or two ago would have dissipated it. He and I were walking on a beach. He had been walking down there earlier in the afternoon, he said, and had seen two sailors making pictures in the sand with a stick. They made a boat he liked, then they made a woman. 'I didn't like that,' he added. 'You wouldn't have liked it either.'

John is still very fond of fairy stories and he has always been a spinner of yarns himself, all kinds of yarns, and for the audience of his contemporaries they are never too silly or too rambling for they always have the unexpected in them. One day when he was about seven years old I was sitting near him, inconspicuous but within earshot of the story he was telling. The two boys listening to him were even more entertained than usual; but this time his subject was not happy. It was an extremely childish but yet unmistakable attempt at obscenity – reminding me a little of Anatole France. (Let me say that the vocabulary I had taught him and the knowledge I had given him did not enter into it at all.) I said nothing to John at the time, but that evening I remarked to him that I had happened to overhear his afternoon story and that I was surprised by its vulgarity and its *dulness*. It was not up to his mark. It was a stupid subject for a story. He would choose better next time, I hoped. The very next afternoon the stage was set in the same way. I was in the same place, in my sun parlor, and the three boys on top of the shed looking on the street. 'Tell us another story, John, just like the one you told

---

[13] Elsie Parsons' eldest boy was also named John.

yesterday.' 'No, I don't feel like telling a story today,' rejoined John, 'Let's play water bombs.'

'You didn't handle the situation well at all', said Amos when I told him about it. 'You ought to have interrupted the story and shamed John then and there, telling him how disgusting it was to you.' I wonder. It might have made him more careful not to tell that kind of a story again in my hearing; it might have given him a 'respect' for me; but would it have affected his partiality for the topic – except to give it the additional lure of secrecy? I am not certain.

En route from Lenox to New York, Sept.
'What's become of Félicité S?' I happened to ask the station-master at Stockbridge as I was waiting in that station for a train. She was a Stockbridge girl who had lived a year or more with me as a maid. She was of a French-Canadian-Irish family, young, pretty, and well brought up by her competent French mother. She was joyous enough at times not to belie her name, but her clear eyes were bits of tiger stone and her ideas of caste propriety so impermeable that I really never knew her. She left me to become a clerk in Boston and I quickly lost track of her. 'Félicité! Why, haven't you heard? She got into trouble. It was M. – the Boston lawyer in whose office she worked. She was somewhere in Connecticut when the child was born – this summer. The nurse found it dead in her arms one night with finger prints on its throat. The whole thing was hushed up though. Some people say she is here now and some people say she isn't.' 'Why *did* she kill her child?' We heard the train whistle and I don't know how the station master might have answered my question, a very stupid question. The answer was so apparent. Poor victim of a society cruel from sheer blindness...! I wish Félicité had remembered me. It would have been natural; for she had lived with us the months before the baby I lost was born. Together we might have planned for her child, or else, irreconcilable, she might have been kept in the beginning from becoming an unwilling mother. I would have arranged it for her – in my own house, if necessary.

Sept.
'And he a married man too!' exclaimed a village friend,
giving me her views about the misadventure of Félicité. 'To
think of him committing such a thing on the girl! But I'm
not excusing her either. Just as soon as she found out what
sort of a man he was she ought to have left his office.' It
was the characteristic view of proprietary sex morals, the
girl a victim and yet responsible, a chattel expected to
safeguard its integrity, the relation purely a pursuit.... 'We
had another girl in the village lately who got into trouble.
Such a quiet girl too! But he was a young fellow and could
marry her. He didn't want to marry her though. Her
family too advised her to marry him, all of them, father and
mother and brothers. Her mother said she'd look after the
baby. But the girl was set on marrying him. She said she
wasn't going to have her child without a father. They were
married two weeks before the child was born.' [She was a
fool to marry him, *I* think. Like F. that girl was a friend of
A's (Mrs B's daughter), such a quiet girl too. When N.
(Mrs B's son) heard about it, he wrote to his sister, 'What
are all you girls coming to!']

Sept. 15
Conservative attitudes certainly are at hand here. Today,
for exmple, I heard an old gentleman tell his daughter and
her friend, middle-aged women, not to take the road over
the hills hemming in this valley – it was too lonely a walk
for a Sunday afternoon when men were idle. 'Very well,
Father', says his daughter, and the two women turned off
into the valley highway. 'Very well, Father', had been the
answer of another daughter in another Lenox family when
'unhappily married' her father told her that he did not
believe in divorce. 'Very well, Father...'. The patriarchal
rule still lingers here, showing fewer signs of being hard put
to than in most places. And yet even here it is sometimes
rebelled against. There have been within the year two
elopements[f] – for the classical reason, for the sake of a

---

[f] But an elopement is in itself a *quasi*-recognition of the patriarchate.
E.C.P.

'mixed marriage'. In the first case she was a Catholic, her
parents French Canadians here since youth; he a Protestant,
an immigrant French Swiss. They ran away no further than
our farm road, and he became our head gardener. In the
second case she belonged to a plutocratic Philadelphia
family and he was the village musician. Her family
received much sympathy for several weeks; our acquaintances referred to her mother as 'poor Fannie' and they
paid her visits of condolence. Now I hear the family is
'reconciled'. Our gardener is not yet received by his family-
in-law.

Sept. 16
I walk over our hills far and wide and never meet another
'tramp'. In the valley roads or byroads the passersby are
always civil. Nevertheless the Old Gentleman is not alone
in putting the fear of the Unknown Male into the female
heart. Today I asked Janet on her return from a visit to a
neighbor if she had had a pleasant time.[14] 'Not as much
fun as usual, Mother', she answered. 'Emma's father
wouldn't let us ride around the place. He had some new
workmen, he said, and he didn't know what they were
like.' 'Probably like his old workmen,' I followed up, 'very
nice men.' It was the best I could do at the moment to
counter the suggestion of the bug-a-boo of foreign
masculinity. With some little girls it is never counteracted,
I feel sure. Another neighbor, a contemporary of my own,
tells me that after dusk she never walks from her farm to
the village, a mile away. 'I don't dare – there're so many
foreigners about.' In our little farmhouse we have a
pleasant, comfortable room, our guest room, on the ground
floor and another, much less satisfactory, upstairs. In the
ground floor room my trained nurse has never been willing
to sleep – 'anybody could get in through the window'. And
she is a woman of unusual courage and readiness in
emergencies. She it was who saved her patient, a young

[14] The character of Janet is based on that of Parsons' daughter Elsie
('Lissa').

man, from being burned to death in one of the most notorious of hotel fires by locking the hall door against him and leading him out along the narrow sleetbeaten ridges of the building. Once she nearly sacrificed her life for one of my babies. Just now she is reforming the nurseries of South America, incidentally encountering doctors who diagnose measles as typhoid and baffling kidnappers who have planned to force out the president of the turbulent republic by making his resignation the ransom of one of his children. One night I had another guest who also declined the ground floor guest-room. She was a village bred girl who had the kindness and the pluck to answer my appeal for a foster-baby for a day or two, my own baby being too frail to nurse at that critical moment. And so she came with her month-old baby, – one of the most humane and generous services one woman could render another; but that night and the next, she slept – upstairs....

When I told Amos about the taboo laid by Emma's father, it led to an argument, Amos backing Emma's father. 'Besides, you don't seem to allow for the fact,' Amos wound up, 'that it would be exceedingly repugnant to him to think of his daughter arousing objectionable feelings in his workmen.'[g] I suppose I don't. At any rate I am going to refer to Emma's father in the paper I am to read soon to a Woman's Club at Santa Fe on Nursery Bug-a-boos.

Sept. 17.
More bug-a-boo data. Janet has another little friend called Alice. She is to lunch with us today, go with Janet to the flower show in the village and then we are to send her home. 'I must drive home with her,' said Janet, 'for her mother doesn't want her to drive alone with anybody's coachman but their own.' 'What a strange idea!' I exclaimed. 'Well, when you go to the flower show together you may drive yourselves and put up the pony in the blacksmith's shed.' Janet: 'Oh, mother, we can't do that

---

[g] An association of sympathetic magic, father and daughter participating in the feelings of the laborers, and infected by them. *E.C.P.*

because Alice's father has told her she mustn't go into a stable and the blacksmith's shed is just the same thing.' Mother: 'What's the matter with the blacksmith's shed?' Janet: 'There's always a lot of men standing around there.' Mother: 'What's the matter with the men?' Janet: 'They might swear – that's what Alice's father says.' Mother: 'And they might not. But what if they do? You don't have to swear because they swear.... But drop Alice at the show and put the pony up yourself.' Janet: 'Please, mother, I'd much rather have the coachman drive us up.'

September 18.
What precautions men will take for the safety of women in some ways, and in some ways only. Today the wife of one of our workmen gave birth to her sixth child. She is under thirty and she is a wreck. I talked about her to her physician, he is mine too, a New York man. 'She's in bad condition', he said. 'After she convalesces we'll put her to rights; but more than anything it's important for her not to have any more children – at least not for three or four years.' 'Will you tell her that?' 'Yes.' 'Will you tell her what precautions to take?' 'No, I can't do that.' 'Pray then, what do you expect will happen?' No answer. 'I'll tell her then.' 'As you like.' Had I told him I was planning to camp out on the mountain alone, let us say, running infinitesimally the risk of what he must have known was almost a certainty for his other patient, the consequences of such a disaster being greatly more serious to her physically too than to me, would he have merely said, 'As you like?' Would he not quite vehemently have protested?

September 29, The South West, Train No. 3, California Limited.
As I was registering yesterday in Chicago for a room between trains, I heard at my side, 'Hello Cynthia!' and there stood —, a New York friend.[15] He seemed, for him, a placid, lazily humorous man, a bit taken aback. It came

[15] 'A New York friend': Kirk Brice. See Zumwalt pp. 151–52.

out in the subsequent comedy we played together in the
hotel ticket office and over my coffee that he thought I was
inviting myself to join an Apache hunt[16] he and —, a
mutual friend, a Chicago newspaper man,[17] were to start
for that night, and oddly enough on my train. We decided
to continue the comedy in league together against – at
lunch. 'It's entirely a question of sex,' said —. 'It's not my
party.... There are three or four other men already out in
Arizona.... What would they say to a woman's coming
along...? I'd go anywhere in the world with you alone. I
know no man a better sport than you, and few able to
stand more or as much.... But the other men don't know
that... Besides men sometimes go on such trips, just to get
away from women...'[h] – plainly had no doubt I wanted to
come. In fact even when both men knew of my own plan,
an expedition more interesting and venturesome than
theirs, it did not seem to occur to them that adventuring in
the Southwest on my own I could find agreeable. They did
seem a little fatuous, and yet it was a natural enough point
of view, however circumscribed, and a very striking
illustration of the implicit belief of the male in the
dependence of the female, a belief assuredly justified.

Later. Somewhere in Kansas.
From asking me about riding clothes – passed to the
consideration of clothes in general. 'Nudity, I believe, has
nothing to do with morality,' he opined, inoculated
evidently with the summer's newspaper and magazine
discussions of the subject. 'Perhaps not' I rejoined, and
then to see if he had really thought it out I added: 'I go
about my own house when we are alone and whenever I

[h] They do, or rather out hunting they feel they must avoid women. In the
Congo Bangala trappers avoid women from the time they make or set
up their trap until the quarry is caught or even eaten. An Uganda
woman who caught an animal of any kind or killed it would be
considered unfit for society. *E.C.P.*

[16] 'Apache hunt.' An Apache deer hunt.

[17] 'A Chicago newspaper man': John McCutcheon, journalist and
cartoonist.

feel like it, without clothes.' 'Before your children? Before your son John?' No, he had *not* thought it out. 'Yes, before John.'[18] 'And how old is John?' 'Ten.' 'Well, I think you are running a great risk. I should be afraid of its hurting his ideal of his mother.'[i] Ah...you do then think of purity as inseparable from clothes and between purity and morality you see, I suppose, some relation....

What manifestations of conjugality a train induces! As a rule it's most openly displayed in the 'diner', where he orders for her and the two eat in silence or drop remarks about the outcome of their order. But this morning a capital example sat on the observation car. It was a prosperous couple, he with a diamond scarfpin and she with pearl earrings, both corpulent, both proprietary. With their knees touching they discussed the time table, gettting slightly irritated with each other. 'Where do you see that?...'. 'I told you so...'. 'That's just like you...'. 'Be careful, you'll tip backwards dear.' 'No I won't.' 'Look out, you're getting your arm covered with cinders.' 'Well, I can't help it...'. With slight variations it was the conversation they had been having with each other for some years and would go on having for many more if they continued to be 'happily married'. It was a simian sort of performance – without physical agility, nor are monkeys, I suppose, ever fat.

On the way from Laguna to Santa Fe, October 1.
'It's cheaper traveling with your wife than without her', said Mr Clack of Gallup, as he motored me back yesterday from Acoma. 'How do you make that out?' I had of course to ask. 'Well, she keeps you from doing foolish things. Besides when you're not with your own wife, you're with

[i] i.e., his representation of his mother. In primitive thought garments or ornament are a part of personality. Their wearer impregnates them with his own nature. Manifestations of 'modesty' which consist of a disinclination to take off clothes may be explained form this point of view. E.C.P.

[18] Parsons argued with Herbert Parsons about the propriety of going without clothes in the presence of their children. See Zumwalt p. 76.

somebody else's.' 'And she costs more?' 'That's it.' Mr
Clack of Gallup was raised in the panhandle of Texas and
was an automobile demonstrator and, let me add, a knight
errant. 'I like to travel with my wife,' he continued, 'when
there's a party of us. But when we're alone together, she
doesn't make friends with strangers, like I do.' It was quite
evident he did. He did with me.... Walking down the steep
trail from the *mesa* the Mexican [Jew friend of his who was
along with] Mr C. suggested a bottle of beer – they had a
'lunch' with them in the motor, for we had come eighteen
miles out from Laguna that afternoon and the hour of
return was uncertain. 'No beer until we're back', I said
with a laugh. (The road was as adventurous for a motor as
Fifth Avenue or the trail of the Grand Cañon for a horse.)
'I drink dozens of bottles of beer a day,' protested Clack, 'I
have to in my business. It doesn't affect me in the least...'.
As we reached the motor his friend held out a bottle to
him. Clack glanced at me. 'No,' he said, seeing me still
uncompromising, 'give me a cigarette. I won't drink it. I
know how you feel.' Later I remarked to him that a New
Yorker or an Englishman would have said I was a fool and,
having made me believe it, drunk the beer. 'I believe in
being a gentleman,' he rejoined. 'Yes, but after all there're
different ways of being a gentleman. And I *was* a fool.' He
too understood the art of compliment. 'You're the most
romantic woman I ever met', was his way of telling me that
my imagination had been fitly stirred by that amazing *mesa*
of Acoma and its history. As I paid him off he gave me one
of those bottles of beer (knowing I had little prospect of
supper at the section house where I was to spend the night)
and an invitation to visit him and his wife at Gallup. 'She's
not a romantic woman herself', he felt it but fair to tell
me....

I fared well, after all, in the section house. A tidy young
New England woman kept house there for a husband and a
little son and served meals to a varying number of railway
men. She was a healthy cheerful body, but the West she
did not like. On the other side of the tracks in the station
building lived a woman who did. She was married to the

Agent and was herself one of the three station telegraph
operators. Her hours were from 7 am to 3 pm. The
unpaid housewife and the wife with a job of her own – did
that economic difference between the two women enter into
their feeling about their place of residence? I saw too little
of them to learn, but one speculated....

As I sat out on the porch of the section house smoking I
was joined by one of the railway 'hands', an elderly man.
He accepted one of my cigarettes civilly and quite simply.
What an extraordinary difference the slightest personal
relation makes. Looking on from the tracks at me smoking
he would have jeered, I have no doubt, like the others.

Santa Fe, Hotel de Vargas.
My paper on 'Nursery Bug-a-boos' seemed to take with the
Woman's Club. From my perorating brief against fear of
rape we passed into 'an experience meeting', always a
compliment to a lecturer, and in this case really grist to my
mill. The president of the club related how when she was a
young married woman in Kansas a man in a buggy drove
up to her farmhouse door to sell scissors. She bought a
pair, and then he asked her to get into his buggy and show
him the way to her father-in-law's farm. She got in and
then became terrified by the thought that the scissor man
meant to kidnap her. Until they took the turning which led
to her father-in-law's and nowhere else she was in a state of
panic. 'It didn't occur to you, I suppose, that your driver
was more interested in his scissors than in you?' someone
put it to her. 'No, indeed', answered Snow White of
Kansas.

'My family lived near Chicago when I was a girl,' another
member spoke up, 'and I went into the city one day to see
my cousins. They had moved and I asked the car
conductor about the address. An old man sitting next to
me said he lived in that street and would show me the way.
But as I had been told never to speak to a stranger or ask a
question in the streets except of a car conductor or a
policeman, I got off the car in a hurry and ran ahead of the
old gentleman. 'You might just as well have gone with

him,' said my uncle later when he heard my story, 'he lives next door to us and only last week he kicked a young man off his porch for being impertinent, as he thought, to his daughter.' 'I think it was just as well you *didn't* go with the old gentleman', went on another member. 'Once when I was about sixteen I sat for three hours in the station in Chicago, too frightened to ask a direction of anybody until I thought of asking the ticket man. The telegram to my relatives had not reached them. I think girls ought to feel that way about speaking to strangers. I think our daughters today are much too independent for their own good. Fear is a protection.' 'It's costly though and not always necessary,' said a woman sitting near her. 'After I was married we lived on a ranch in Idaho. I was alone most of the day so I asked my husband to give me a pistol. 'What do you want with a pistol?' 'Oh, a drunken tramp might come along some time.' So he gave me the pistol. One day an old tramp *did* come along and he *was* drunk. 'Do you see those silk socks?' he asked me as I opened the door. 'I've got six more pair just like those at home, all silk. Can I sharpen your husband's razor?' 'No,' I said, 'he keeps it locked up, but here are two kitchen knives which need sharpening.' So he took them down to the barn -- in a zigzag course – and sharpened them. When he came back he told me he was born in Florida, in my own country, so we talked about it quite a while and I gave him some lunch. 'Well,' he said, 'I must be going, but I'd like to stay longer and meet your husband. I'd like to see the man who could entice such a girl from Florida to this godforsaken place.' 'What' said my husband that evening, 'you gave a drunken old tramp knives to sharpen and a lunch and spent most of the afternoon talking to him! [He was really mad.] 'What about that pistol?' 'Oh, I forgot all about the pistol.' 'You aren't fit to be trusted', said my husband.

'When I first came here,' said a very old lady, 'the Santa Fe girls used to walk all over the hills by themselves without any fear of the Indians or Mexicans. 'But then, several years ago, two girls were robbed and another girl was murdered on the hills. Since then we don't allow the

girls to walk outside the town.' 'Yes,' said a woman next
to the old lady, 'there're so many convicts working on the
roads.' The ladies had to be answered. 'I always thought
convicts working on the roads were guarded.... Young men
are sometimes robbed and murdered, but we don't keep
our boys in constant fear of assault.'

Afterwards at tea I had a heart-to-heart talk with another
old lady. 'I can't talk before people,' she said, 'besides I
know nobody would agree with me. But it seems to me the
less girls know the better. My son-in-law, a physician, said
to me after my daughter's marriage, 'I didn't suppose any
girl could know so little.' 'Aren't you glad you have such
an innocent wife?' I said to him...I was past forty before I
knew anything about venereal disease, and then I wondered
if every man I met had it. It was horrid. Well brought up
girls have a natural instinct anyway against taking risks.
But I know nobody agrees with me any more.'

Pajarito Ranch, New Mexico, October 12.
Back from my nine days' ride through the White Horse
Cañon of the Rio Grande up over the broken mesas to
Cochite, to San Fernando, to Sant' Anna, to Zia, to —, and
back through the — Forest – a magical country of
mountains and tablelands and *arroyos* and make-believe
deserts and a sky that plays no end of parts all at the same
time, such skies! Pedro Baca, my Indian guide from Santa
Clara,[19] and I slept out in our blankets – twice when we
mistrusted the trail – or in the house of an Indian host. A
Pueblo house or rather the family division of their great
community building consists usually of two rooms, the
living and sleeping room and a store room in which there
may be a sizeable fireplace for cooking. Once my mattress
was spread out for me in the storeroom – that was rather a
piece of luck for it gave me a chance to look at the
ceremonial masks and rattles and head pieces hung above

[19] Like the encounter with Mr Clack of Gallup, and the meeting with Brice
and McCutcheon, this account of an expedition in the company of
Pedro Baca is clearly based on Parsons' own 1910 trip to New Mexico,
and on subsequent visits when she stayed with Pueblo families.

my head – but in the other houses I slept in the common room. Morning and evening and at odd times during the two days when we were exploring nearby ruins, I had opportunities to observe the family life. Pedro Baca I may say always introduced me as his good friend, not a mere white woman, and I seemed to cause no restraint.... How much and how little sex enters into the Pueblos' life – it appears to count very little if at all in their personal relations, but in their occupations it is all controlling. The men farm, get and cut wood, tend the horses and cattle and sheep; the women fetch water, often a laborious undertaking, so steep are the trails to the source of supply or so long, make the fires, and prepare and serve the food. Were a man even to touch the cooking utensils he thinks he would lose his sense of the trail, one young wife educated in American schools, told me, implied criticism in her voice. The women are also the house plasterers and the potters. The men are the tanners and weavers. Men and women belong to different 'Societies', those secret organizations in which their non-familial social life and their religion [outside of the family] are centred. Husband and wife sleep together on the same floor-spread mattress, otherwise in the large joint-family it was difficult to learn merely from observation whose husband or wife a man or a woman was, so oblivious of the other was each. One exception I noticed. Married within the year the girl referred to her husband with pride, 'My boy back soon. He speak English.' And she and he were given the store room to sleep in or for her part to giggle in after they had retired for the night. But even this allowance of privacy seemed unusual. Sons and their wives, daughters and their husbands had to fit into the patriarchal family and like children serve their elders. The old people were in complete control. Sons and sons-in-law did not smoke in the presence of their father, and daughters and daughters-in-law made their kind little overtures to me behind their mother's back....

The Pueblos are monogamous, were so even before Catholicism was thrust upon them. They are strict monogamists too, strongly disapproving of 'irregularities'.

Temia's story is in evidence. Temia, an orphan, had been married at fourteen to a widower of thirty-five. He drank and he beat her. Her three babies died and at last she was allowed by the Indian council to leave her husband. At the end of ten years or more of celibacy Antonio falls in love with her and she with him. The Catholic priest does not approve of them nor the Federal Indian Agent nor the Pueblo Council. Nevertheless they set up housekeeping together and this year I see the seed corn hanging outside of their house wall, the token of one expected. A month or so ago Temia had to be summoned on some public matter before the Council. As she stepped into the council room, all the councillors wrapped their heads in their blankets – [lest] 'other Indian might do same thing' – (and the country be ruined by its divorce rate).

The Indian Agent who has been refusing his consent to a legal divorce for Temia has lately greatly incensed my hostess[20] because he wanted to rent from her a little adobe house on the borders of her ranch for a friend who was more than a friend – or less. 'Why doesn't he keep her in the Red Light District of Santa Fe!' she exclaimed. 'What impudence to thrust her under our noses!' 'Having a high opinion of your company,' I observed, 'remembering how hospitable you were towards him here one summer, perhaps he wanted his friend to have a nice time with you too. After all isn't that rather a decent idea?'

[20] 'My hostess...'. Possibly Mabel Dodge Luhan (1879–1962). A friend whom Parsons had known in New York, she was a wealthy society hostess and supporter of liberal causes. In 1922 she married Antonio Lujan, a Pueblo native American, and settled in her husband's community in Taos, where she and Lujan worked for native American rights. They also hosted writers and artists, among them D.H. Lawrence.

Surprisingly, although she comments on the indignation of her hostess that the Indian Agent had brought his mistress to stay in the pueblo community, Parsons does not discuss the Agent's hypocrisy in conducting this affair while refusing the request for remarriage of a divorced Pueblo woman.

East of La Junta, October 15.

And, I might have added, an idea requiring courage to entertain – considering. Considering too the domination of the point of view I have just beeen observing in this car. He is about thirty, well dressed, looks well-bred. She, from thirty to forty, nicely but not smartly dressed, not pretty, but her voice cultivated and engaging. She has a foreign accent and too much vitality, psychical vitality, for an American woman. It was her foreign quality that first attracted my attention to them, then it was arrested by the fact that they were flirting each other, a really uncommon sight [on a train, or perhaps in any public place] in this country of wretched sex taboos. She began it of course, but he was enjoying it – until quite accidentally I came on the scene. They were given seats at my table in the dining-car. He caught sight of my Phi Beta Kappa key and had to ask me where I got it. Columbia was his university too, I saw from his glance at her, and he too had been a lecturer there. His questions made any by me superfluous. But it soon became obvious he was afraid I was going to ask questions. As the idea grew in his mind he became more and more uncomfortable, and his pleasure in her went. I was glad to leave the table for her sake. She was too much of a lady not to see he was [acting or rather feeling like] a cad. Perhaps though she had already labelled him for herself as a typical American, fearful of pleasure and furtive. It is the type that in certain circles makes the red light district possible or 'necessary', and, in others, verses like those of Alice Meynell's[21] on Renunciation (?) popular.

---

[21] Alice Meynell's 'Renunciation'. Alice Meynell, poet and essayist, (1847–1922). The poem Parsons probably has in mind is actually titled, 'Renouncement'. It reads in part:

> Oh, just beyond the fairest thoughts that throng
> This breast, the thought of thee waits hidden yet bright;
> But it must never come in sight;
> I must stop short of thee the whole day long...'

Alice Meynell, Prose and Poetry. Eds. F.P., V.M., O.S. and F.M.

With a biographical and critical introduction by V. Sackville-West. London: Cape, 1947.

East of Kansas City, October 18.
'When will they provide smoking cars for ladies?' [a
faithful campaigner,] I have just been asking my Pullman
conductor, standing near him on the platform and
snatching a smoke. 'When the ladies vote,' he answered. 'A
lady enjoys a smoke as much as a man. She has a perfect
right to. This is a free country. But they won't get
smoking cars until they vote...'. It was as curious a
sequence of ideas as that expressed to me the other day in
Santa Fe by an [American] archeologist of my
acquaintance. He said he had lately become a woman
suffragist because he had learned that an Englishman could
introduce his mistress into his wife's house with perfect
impunity, legal impunity I suppose he meant. Thinking
only that more than one trail may lead up to the same
divide, I had no rejoinder for him, but I rather wished for
the fun of the thing that Miss —, one of the apple pickers
of Pajarito Ranch, had been with us. She is the young
daughter of a Colorado Mormon bishop. Lately her father
has taken another wife. 'Only very good women are
contented to be a plural wife', was her comment upon his
present household. Yes, only women without vanity or
pettiness or selfishness and – *perhaps*, without imagination.[22]

Lenox, October.
I trained today to Chatham, meeting Herbert there on the
New York train. We walked over the hills ten miles or so to
an inn the little newspaper girl in the station had glowingly
recommended to me as I was waiting for Herbert's train.
We reached it about four, to unconcealed disapproval of its
proprietress, a fat and unyielding female. So cross and
unyielding that altho' she gave us the meal we were two
hours late for, we had to eat it in our wet boots. Although

[22] Parsons herself suffered painfully from jealously of Herbert Parsons'
affair with Lucy Wilson. Parsons expressed admiration for the seeming
freedom of her friend Alice Duer Miller from such emotions. '[S]he
doesn't really know what jealousy is like', Parsons wrote. See Zumwalt
p. 83.

there were no other guests in the house, she couldn't say about our spending the night there until her husband came back. Finally we 'passed' and were given rooms. Herbert came into mine and sat for an hour or more in the rockingchair, smoking and talking and reading aloud to me, as I lay down resting, [an amusing skit...in Harper's]. Then he went downstairs to the sitting room of the proprietress to ask about having his boots dried and cleaned. In a few minutes he returned to report that the proprietor, an Irish American, had asked him with much embarrassment, to please not sit in my room. 'We don't think you're that sort of people, still we have to be careful.' What a point of view. Irritating of course at the time because practically inconvenient; but interesting now, for isn't it to be added to my collection of cases of contagious magic? The evil we might have wrought were we 'that sort of people' – evil undoubtedly in their eyes and that point we needn't take up – would have been contaminating, [not considering the circumstances to the reputation of the house, but to themselves, actually, positively.]

October 31.
We are to have a Hallowe'en party. Janet has planned it all, consulting me only on moot points. One of them has arisen over a difference in point of view between her and John in their conception of the role of host. We are to have a prize for the winner of the competition in pinning on the donkey's tail. Now if she or John happen to win, should either keep the prize, being host? 'I will,' says John, 'It's fair.' 'I won't,' says Janet, 'It would be inhospitable. I'd give it to the littlest child.' 'You needn't go into the event at all, if you like,' I suggest, 'but if you do and win, perhaps the guests would rather you kept the prize, perhaps they'd prefer to have you treat them as competitors to the end.' 'Yes, they would,' says John. 'No, they wouldn't,' says Janet. And the matter hangs until an aunt appearing is appealed to. Feeling her support, Janet is emboldened in her argument. 'Even if the children didn't mind, their mothers wouldn't like it,' she goes on. 'But it might be a

good thing for their mothers to get a new idea about it,' I rejoin. 'They wouldn't let their children come here again,' urges Janet, 'would they, Aunt Maggie?' 'They might not,' answers Aunt Maggie. 'Surely, Maggie, you don't think that even if the mothers disagreed they'd attach enough importance to the incident to keep their children away another time?' 'Yes, I do. It's just one of those things mothers are particular about.' And so Janet triumphs. A little later she triumphs again. She is showing us the regulation symbols for the cake – ring and coin and thimble. 'What's the thimble for ?' asks John. 'For industry and skill,' I put in quickly. 'Mother, you know it's for the Old Maid,' protests Janet. 'No one wants to get it. All the children know it's for the Old Maid. You can't change it, can you Aunt Maggie?' Maggie is not an old maid, she is an arrogant young mother; but she has a spinster sister, Jane, a very dear sister. 'I suppose not. Your aunt Jane got the thimble last night in a cake,' she laughs, 'and we all thought it a good joke, it was so appropriate.' 'Is Aunt Jane an old maid?' asks John. Aunt Maggie would sacrifice much for Jane – but Aunt Maggie is also a pillar of society. And so the discrediting of Jane to her nephew seems appropriate. Only of course Maggie doesn't put it that way. She doesn't put it to herself at all, I surmise. She just passes on the tradition – like other mothers. And yet she is bringing up her children on the Montessori method, and she is known as an 'advanced' woman.[i]

November.
I dined out last night – orchids, terrapin soup, footmen in breeches, a carefully careless hostess – that sort of thing. I sat between two fathers of daughters and of daughters only. The elder, old enough to be my father, had been

---

[i] Jokes on old maids are played even among savages – when there are old maids to play them on. It was considered a good practical joke among the Blackfeet for the young men to lasso and overturn at night the tipi of some elderly spinster. Her tipi jerked away there she would be left sitting frightened and mortified by her sudden exposure to public view. (McClintock, pp. 298–9) E.C.P.

reading Wells' 'last' novel, the story of a man's life written
out by him for the benefit of his son. 'Rather a curious
idea,' said Mr F.... 'I believe in parents trying to pass on
their experience, but there're some things they can't talk
about – no gentleman could.' Recognizing that formula as
one invariably intended to close discussion[k] I complaisantly
diverged. 'Would you be franker about life in general with
a son than with a daughter?' I asked. 'Yes, to be sure[l]
although my daughters and I have been very good friends.'
At this moment, the lady on my right exacting attention, I
turned to him on my left, Emma's father. 'Would you talk
to Emma about everything as freely as if she were a boy?' I
asked him. 'Yes, our American girls whisper and giggle
over subjects no European woman young or old would
think of taking that way. I don't like it.' I forgot to ask
why he was making Emma so suspicious of the Unknown
Male. He soon gave me an answer to that unuttered
question, however, by a question of his own. Did I never
meet with 'any unpleasantness' in traveling alone in the
Southwest? Obviously he was making Emma afraid of the
Unknown Male because he was himself afraid.... So I had
to tell him about Mr Clack of Gallup and his gallantry. I
followed it up too with a story about Long John. Long
John, a much quoted man along the upper Rio Grande,
was, when I met him, the driver of a coach between – and
Taos. Only that day he was to take me the sixteen miles in
a buggy. At — another passenger left the train with me –
evidently a commercial traveler and evidently somewhat
questionable. As Long John drove up to the the shanty that
did for a station, the 'traveling man' in a sniveling sort of
way asked me if he couldn't get a lift in the buggy, sitting
behind. I referred him to Long John. 'No, I've got no
room for you,' Long John snapped out at the man, adding
to me as we drove off, 'He can't get to Taos on this trip.
He'll have to sit here until the next train comes along. It's
due tomorrow morning at ten, but it's apt to be late. He's

[k] Quite so; it is one of our taboo formulas. *E.C.P.*

[l] A modified form of the practice of avoidance. Elsewhere the impulse
expresses itself more crassly. *E.C.P.*

a bum. He's half drunk now. He's not fit to drive in the same carriage with a lady.' 'Long John is unique in New Mexico in many ways,' I concluded, 'but not in sparing a lady any unpleasantness.'

New York, Nov. 12.
'I'm going to a talky-talky dinner tonight on mothers' pensions', I remarked yesterday to Amos in for tea. 'Why we don't take warning from our war pension history I don't understand,' said Amos, 'there'll be the same fraud and cost.' 'If you could have all our war pensions converted by magic into mothers' pensions, would you?' 'No, you have to have war pensions to have soldiers.' 'Perhaps you have to have mothers' pensions to have citizens – for peace or war.' 'No, pensioning wouldn't affect the birthrate in the least. Women have children anyhow. They have to.' 'Do they?' But I let pass, and handing him his cup of tea I resumed with: 'You don't believe in mothers' pensions then?' 'Some time perhaps when we know more about eugenics we might have a limited system of pensions as a sort of prize money for especially fine children.' I was rather persistent – one sometimes has to be with Amos. 'How about the question from an economic point of view? Do you think a woman ought to be economically dependent on a man during childbearing?' 'Yes.' Amos paused, a little irritated, 'but I wouldn't put it that way.' 'How would you put it?' I really was curious. 'The family ought to provide for the occasion.'

New York, November.
At the last moment I was sidetracked from the public dinner to a private and far pleasanter party. Nevertheless the subject of mothers' pensions was not altogether sidetracked for me that evening. It came up in a talk with M. – on illegitimacy [the editor of a popular magazine]. How bemuddled he is on questions of sex and how – representative. Last night he was voicing a conception very prevalent, I think, among men, the conception that but for law men would be regardless of paternity and altogether

promiscuous. They are fathers and husbands only under
the club of society. Let society lay its club aside and the
male brute will ramp. 'Because of the physical superiority
of men and because of the lust that is in them,' M. asserted,
'women have benefitted on the whole from the laws of
marriage, and from the taboos of sex.' Seeing [that I
couldn't or] I wouldn't try to meet so comprehensive an
assertion, he undertook to specify. 'What would you do
about a man say of forty-five who, because he knows all
the tricks, succeeds in enticing a girl say of nineteen, and
then deserts her and their child?' 'Nothing much happens
to the man now, of course,' I answered, 'but you think I
suppose many more men of forty-five would become
irresponsible but for the institution of marriage?' 'Yes.'
'I'm not so sure.... But what would I have happen in the
case you bring up? I'd have the child bear the name of
both his father and his mother, just as all children will,
once we are quite free of the theory of paternal descent.
Nor should the fact of the man's paternity be in any way
concealed. It need not be on the girl's account. For neither
she nor the child should be penalized – by society. Her lack
of foresight or restraint brings its own punishment – in her
disappointment in the child's father. Isn't that a harsh
enough experience? As for him, in so far as he is
unscrupulous, let those around him know it, that they may
be on their guard against him. As it is, the public has no
way of protecting itself against him. He can go on
'deceiving' other girls, or rather shirking the responsibility
of paternity. There's no *law* against illegitimacy now, and
yet see how strong the social pressure is upon the woman
who 'gets into trouble' as childbearing under these circumstances is so pleasingly called. Let the pressure be directed
against the unpaternal man. Let there be a State pension
for the mother. That would direct public disapproval
against the irresponsible father. The tax-paying public
would in course of time disapprove of the men who shifted
upon it their own responsibilities...'.[23] Was not M's query

[23] 'men...shifted...responsibilities...'. Parsons would have deplored the
enactment of legislation like that passed in Britain in the 1990s, which
required the single mother to identify the absent father as an integral
part of the process of assessing her eligibility for state financial
assistance.

a first class illustration of how befuddling the questions of sex relations and of parenthood, if unseparated, may be, always are in fact? 'I believe in institutional marriage', M had said. In reality it was in institutional parenthood he believed. But belief in institutional parenthood, the holding of parents, mothers and fathers, by law or by public opinion, to the obligation of rearing their children, appears to be inseparable in the minds of most persons from a belief in institutional marriage, the determination by outsiders of what purports to be the most intimate of relations between two adult persons. Until these two relations are clearly distinguished in the social mind, there will continue to be a baffled and perverse public opinion on most questions of marriage and of parenthood.[24] To make this distinction clear may be therefore the most important propaganda ahead of us....

The truth is society is not yet alive to the fact that conception can be controlled. The meaning of this momentous new condition in life is not grasped at all. As soon as we do take it in there will be absolutely no excuse for confusing the facts of sex with the facts of parenthood. A demarcation of these two groups of facts would simplify both ethics and life enormously – would we let it.

November.
F. dined with me last night. He has a new 'widow', his generic and from his point of view expressive and histor-ically correct, term for lady-love. This particular lady he was kissing the other night in her house in Philadelphia, he told me, when the servant came into the room. It was very awkward. He had never been caught that way before altho' he had taken chances no end of times. 'It was worse for her, poor woman,' remarked F. with a snicker, 'and I suggested to her to tell the servants I was trying to marry her.' 'What did she say to that?' I asked. 'She said she could hardly take them into her confidence.' F. believes firmly in marriage, and I know no layman so opposed to

----

[24] See Parsons' article, 'When Mating and Parenthood are...Theoretically Distinguished', *International Journal of Ethics*, 26 (1916): pp. 207–16.

freer divorce or so content with the relations as they are between the sexes. He is, I suppose, the most immoral person of my acquaintance. His amazing, unblushing confidences fill me with horror and make me – giggle. They are too depraved to take seriously – and too conventional.

November.
A reporter on one of the evening papers called me up today on the telephone. A girl thirteen years old and a man much older, a man too illiterate to sign his name, had been married in the Mayor's Bureau. 'Wasn't it deplorable?' Wouldn't I express an opinion about it? 'I do not care to express opinions on individual cases; I am not in that business, if there is such a business.' It was the reporter's emphasis of the man's illiteracy which irritated me, I suppose. Otherwise I might just as well have dropped a platitude or two on the absurdity of having the age at marriage below the age of consent.

New York, November.
H.G. Wells does stir people up.... Ethel has been reading *The Passionate Friends* too.[25] Ethel is a woman about thirty-five, with children, a husband and a lover, and so her comment on the book was naturally different from Mr F's. Her grievance was not against the man who lacked in verbal reserve, but against the woman who lacked in physical. 'Lady Mary was a selfish creature, of course, but what I can't forgive her was her surrender to her husband. How could she have lived with him!' 'Lady Mary couldn't help being an old-fashioned woman. She rebelled only in spots. It's always the half rebels who suffer and make others suffer, particularly the half rebels in sex.' Ethel is a

---

[25] H.G.Wells' *The Passionate Friends* indicts the institution of marriage as a destroyer of authentic personal relationships. The main woman character Mary Justin is driven to suicide by marriage to a man she does not love. She has refused to marry the man she really cares for, believing that to confine this relationship within a conventional marriage relation would be to destroy it.

half rebel herself, but I of course did not press home my point. She gave me a cup of tea – we were sitting in her Fifth Avenue drawingroom – and then after we had smoked awhile and expressed our liking for the Stage Society's last play, *The Countess Mietze*, Ethel reverted to the unfortunate Lady Mary. 'But could you live with one man if you were in love with another, or could you even conceive of living with two men at the same time?' 'Perhaps, given our society. Its typical husband wants so very little that it might be easy to gratify him from mere affection. Besides living with a man, as you put it, may be such an indifferent, mechanical kind of performance. A few minutes of passivity now and then. If a man wants no more [than that], he gets no more.' 'But is not physical intimacy a base thing unless it means more than that?' Ethel was very earnest. 'Shouldn't it always be an expression of one's highest feelings?' 'I don't know. Actually of course we know it isn't. In the same relationship too it differs from time to time enormously. Why should we have such fixed preconceptions about one of our senses?' The realization that I was shocking her a little made me even more contrary. 'I wonder sometimes if we don't greatly exaggerate the meaning of physical intimacy. I rather think it's still a stronghold of those theories of contagious magic Elsie Parsons talks about so much,[m] the theories which make the savage believe that all kinds of attributes and qualities pass from one to another through contact, that one controls or masters another through a mere touch. And then except for analogous reasons why should one part of the body be more taboo, more 'sacred', more inviolable than another?' To this tirade I got no answer. Nor did I expect one. Ethel has institutionalized her lover quite as thoroughly as once she did her husband. She has merely shifted the same set of preconceptions from one man to the other. Most women do that – and most men. The lover is still quite as conventional a figure as the husband. He would be a husband if

[m] I suppose I do. The knowledge of their existence is illuminating. They are the source of so many of our confusions of thought. *E.C.P.*

he could. He runs away with another man's wife only because a honeymoon with her is out of the question. A woman may be taken out to dinner by her lover, but not by her husband. She may be kissed by her husband in a railroad station, but not by her lover. In either situation has the physical contact or the lack of it any personal meaning?

November 27.

I drove in Central Park yesterday afternoon with Ernest,[26] my crippled friend who has the art of that talk that can be so intimate because it is so impersonal. He practises it at times by putting to me a query on some subject he seems to have a trick of knowing you have been thinking about. And so yesterday as we turned into one of the Park's haphazard entrances, he suddenly came out with: 'Cynthia, isn't permanent monogamy the best of all relationships after all?' It was the sort of disconnected question that turns one into an oyster, or rather a scallop – a scallop snaps together its shell less quietly than an oyster – except when E. is the questioner. 'Perhaps it is, if I understand what you mean by permanent monogamy. Do you mean an enduring relationship, many-sided and intimate and in so far as it is passionate, exclusive?' 'Yes.' 'That is, I think, the best that can come to one speaking for oneself. But there are so few facts to go upon in generalizing for society. For that kind of relationship has never been tried out by society. The institution of marriage imposes conditions fatal to passion. Because a man knows he can get what he wants at any time he stops taking trouble to get it. And then before he knows it, he can't get it. His uncourted wife has become a passive, passionless woman, at best only a friend, at worst a jealous proprietress. The institution of adultery, the complementary institution to marriage and mind you quite as much of an institution, kills passion too, although in different ways – by fear and

---

[26] Ernest. A character based on Randolph Bourne (1886–1918), social
  critic and pacifist. Bourne was a strong admirer of Parsons' work.

furtiveness and endless restrictions. In both marriage and adultery courtship is hindered or precluded by circumstance. In marriage conditions are too easy; in adultery they are too difficult. Marriage includes everything but passion, adultery excludes everything except passion. So there you are. Love at its best between a man and a woman is really not recognized at all by society. It never has been. So that it has no standards or norm or code.' 'But individuals have worked out standards.' 'Yes, individuals for themselves as best they could. Besides there are the novelists. They've been contributing something to new social conceptions of passion. That is why writers like Meredith and Wells and Galsworthy are attacked as immoral. They are stigmatized as 'suggestive', and they are suggestive. They mean to be. The more *suggestive* they are, the better. They want us to see life as it is, so that we may base our conduct on facts, not on dogma, traditions, preconceptions. Of course, like all moralists they are apt to furnish a set of new preconceptions. Still as yet at any rate they are far less dogmatic than the moralists they are supplanting, priest and legislator and vice-hunters at large.' [We passed on at this point to the disasters of preconception; but I have been thinking again about the social function of the novelist. The mask he wears, for the most part unwittingly, amuses us. It is only when he throws it aside deliberately, challengingly, and writes 'with a purpose' that he is seriously disputed. And he deserves to be, and not alone for aesthetic reasons. As a social leader he ought to preserve his strategic advantages, maintaining the fiction of his being merely a *divertissement*, a dispenser of frivolity and unreality. In reality he is *the* searcher after reality, the social reformer *par excellence*, or he may be.] It's no mere coincidence, is it, that woman has become both the unrestful sex and the novel-reading sex? [The parent of a past generation who when he exacted of his son a promise not to smoke or drink until he became 'of age' threw in for full measure a promise not to read novels was from his own standpoint a wise man indeed.] No, it's no mere coincidence – at least no more of one than that those little boys over there – we were passing that most successful of park ponds at Seventy-second street – should be sailing their boats on the only water accessible to them.

November 28.
Ernest not only makes one talk, he makes one write. [I suppose he stimulates in one a desire for clearness of expression whether in spoken or in written words. At any rate] I have gone on talking [to him since I left him and I'd like just now to write] out my monologue to him. It is about marriage, but it is even more about the emancipation of women, not nearly as trite a subject as it looks. For it seems to me that women are just as unemancipated – in spirit – as ever they were. As far as institutions go, they are of course comparatively free, free enough at any rate to begin to seek for real freedom. Hitherto feminists have been so impressed by the institutional bondage of women, by their disqualifications as property holders, as parents, as citizens, that questions of inner freedom have rarely occurred to them. That is why many of the objective, customary signs of the lack of it have not troubled them, checks upon going about alone, clothes that hinder movement, censorship of ideas and feeling, endless little sex taboos.

Women have been charged with achieving their institutional freedom through a process of unsexing themselves. The charge is generally too vaguely put to be met and too desperate an argument to escape being ludicrous; but nevertheless the charge is just – in itself. To get their institutional rights women have felt that they had to detach themselves from men. The only way they knew to independence was aloofness. And aloofness inevitably engenders antagonism. Sex antagonism has undoubtedly been a characteristic of feminism.

Ignoring the problems of sex has also been a characteristic of the movement. For propaganda against a double code of sex morals like the campaign for suffrage is merely a demand for institutional equality, to being equally subject to the disapproval of society. Even the present crusades against prostitution and venereal disease are essentially efforts for a better social hygiene and a less insincere democracy. On sex problems they do not bear directly at all. Venereal disease might be wiped out without affecting the existence of prostitution and prostitution might go on unrecruited by the victims of trickery or of poverty. The needs of sex which prostitution so inadequately attempts to meet the public has not yet begun seriously to consider.

The problem of sex feminists have now to face is primarily a psychological problem. How are women to live *with* men, not *without* men like the ruthless fighters for institutional freedom, and not in the old way *through* men. The old way is the easy, self-indulgent way. For there seems to be a marked impulse to subjection in the normal woman. Self-surrender is one of the dominant characters of her passion, a delight to her and to her lover, at their supreme moments a natural and unfeigned delight; but from those moments it tends to spread over the whole of a woman's life and to become both a conventionality and a curse, a curse to both man and woman. Her continuous self-surrender persuades him that she is his for the asking or for less. He takes her for granted. Then of course her moment of tragedy begins – to end, like as not, inarticulately and in resignation. As for him, he finally appreciates that she has come to humor him and that her self-surrender is no longer the expression of desire but a mere habit. Thereafter passion is impossible for either, whatever the outward relationship they see fit to maintain. Married or unmarried they have ceased to be lovers.

Marriage facilitates this conclusion in every way; for it encourages self-surrender in a wife, institutionally and practically, institutionally because identification with another is at all turns expected of her, practically because of the close companionship such identification involves. In such close companionship a woman in love rarely withstands the urgency of sex. In truth "Tis woman's whole existence'.[27]

---

[27] '... whole existence.' A quotation from Byron's *Don Juan*:

Man's love is of man's life a thing apart,

Partly to meet this situation, a situation sometimes hard
on a man, and partly from a merely humanitarian spirit
women have been urged for a century or so to become
educated, to acquire intellectual interests. It has been felt
too in an obscure sort of way that an educated woman may
be more companionable than an uneducated woman. It is,
they see, to the advantage of man. And it is to their
advantage too along the same old lines they are accustomed
to. 'Intellectual interests' make a woman more self-
sufficient of course when she is not in love. When she is,
they merely enable her, just like child-bearing, to make her
devotion to another more complete. Against passion
'intellectual interests' are not compelling.

What is compelling, or rather shall we say, disciplinary
for love? Work is, I suppose, intellectual work or indeed
any work that is interesting and exacting. Hitherto the
work of a woman has been considered only from the
economic standpoint, or from the point of view of making
her economically independent of men, a part of the institutional concern of the feminist. It is time now to consider
her work as a safeguard of her spiritual independence – a
preservative of her integrity, a means of discipline. It is
only through work one can be quite sure one is taking life
at first hand and it is only by taking life at first hand, by
being the spiritual equal of her lover that a woman may
preserve a free and passionate life with him, a life of mutual
joys and satisfactions, a life aglow through their
imagination.

Let us turn away from the antiquated advocacy of work
in lieu of love, as an alternative to love, and let us look to
work for the sake of love, as a means of salvation for
love.... I would also like to see tried out pragmatically the
experiment of not necessarily living with the beloved, ie not

'Tis woman's whole existence...

(*Don Juan*, ed. Isaac Asimov, Garden City, New York: Doubleday,
1972: p. 141.)

Clearly, though Parsons recognizes that for many women love may be
an exclusive concern, she also deplore such narrowness of perspective.

keeping house with him or her. Godwin realized that continually living under the same roof together might spoil marriage and so he denied himself the unbroken familiarity of bed and board with Mary Wollstonecraft.[28] But Godwin would be considered as much of a crank today, I suppose, at least in this country, as he was a hundred years ago in England.

New York, December.
That monstrous alternative of the Nineteenth Century, Work-instead-of-Love, is by no means slain. I was talking today to one of the [most faithful and long-serving] secretaries of Barnard College. 'I'm advising girls to go into business,' she said, 'and to stick to it. If I were an employer engaging a girl one of my first questions would be, 'Have you a sweetheart?' I wouldn't take a green girl and break her in to find she was working only for a trousseau.' I laughed. The question she put into the mouth of the would be practical employer seemed so naive and so futile. 'Why not meet the situation in a little different way. Why not ask your applicant, 'Will you throw up your job when you marry? Or will you only go on working on a shorter day if I can arrange one for you?' I went on then to my committee meeting, but I have been thinking since of the Barnard secretary's question and of the substitute I suggested and of how radically different in their implications the two were. Industrial celibacy and race suicide were back of hers; the providing of part time work for women, back of mine. This provision by employers of

[28] 'Godwin...with Mary.' William Godwin (1756–1836), English social philosopher, and Mary Wollstonecraft (1759–1797), pioneer feminist, author of *A Vindication of the Rights of Woman*, were the parents of Mary Shelley, author of *Frankenstein*. Of the decision of Wollstonecraft and Godwin to live in separate apartments during their married life Godwin wrote, '...though, for the most part, we spent the latter half of each day in one another's society, yet we were in no danger of satiety. We seemed to combine in a considerable degree, the novelty and lively sensation of a visit, with the more delicious and heart-felt pleasures of domestic life.'
See *Collected Novels and Memoirs of William Godwin,* ed. Mark Philip, London: Pickering, 1992.

a half day or three quarter day for women who are married or more logically, actual or expectant childbearers, is the vital question, the only vital question left in the subject of women as wage earners. It is or ought to be a vital question to feminists, to economists and to nationalists with the bee of race suicide in their bonnet. Its solution is necessary to the economic independence of women leading a normal life, to precluding waste, turning the surplus energy of married women from extravagant consumption to productive labor, and to checking the tendency to late marriage in both men and women.

New York, December.
G. and H. have long been talking of getting up a feminist party and last night it actually came off.

They had got together six women, chosen, it was alleged, for their looks, their intelligence, and their tongues, to discuss together the biological effects of feminism to the good or amusement of an outer circle of guests, men and women. At the end of a half hour or so the outer circle was to join in the discussion. When I first heard of the plan I realized it was a case of revolt, they had been driven into the last ditch by their woman-run society. They said they wanted honestly to know what women were after. Really they were taking a stand, trying to claim a little of their passing prerogatives. They wanted to crack the whip again [the women to perform for their amusement]. They denied this motive of course, but I still think it was at the bottom of their hearts, although G. in his opening remarks made out that the revolt was directed not against the ladies having all their own way, but against the 'tired business man' having his, that 'Society' might well become a little quicker witted and that men in general should wake up to what was of so much interest to women. Then we started, or rather I was told to start. I had, I said, two points to make, one rather new, and one rather old, necessarily old. First, that feminism was an expression of the disappearing of fear between men and women. Women were coming out of the places assigned them because they were no longer afraid of men. Nor were men afraid of them. Fear is a depressant. This elimination of sex fears might mean a great increase of buoyancy, passion, and vigor for society. Second, taking feminism as an expression of the economic independence of women it meant or would mean that women would cease marrying for money, 'good providers' would no longer be competed for. The money-making mate would cease to be at a premium. Women would choose the men they found companionable. Men would have to compete together along new lines, and so new traits would be developed or encouraged in them – if there was anything in the law of sexual selection. 'In this process would there not be a danger of men becoming in their turn over-sexed?' queried a woman. 'Do you mean that men might become too agreeable?' she was asked and everyone laughed. 'What do you mean by the economic independence of women?' I was asked. 'I mean the independence due to women being income earners – before and *after* marriage.' 'How can they be income earners after marriage?' 'How can they on part time compete with the men?' 'What is to become of the children?' were the to-be-expected questions to receive the to-be-expected answers: 'Modern economy is proceeding less and less along competitive lines'; 'The children are already largely cared for by others than their mother. And better cared for. At least half of their mother's time goes already to housework or housekeeping or her own amusements, not to her children. By putting her on a half-day working schedule you wouldn't necessarily divert her energy or time from her children.' The talk rambled on along well beaten trails. Were married women income earners, men could afford to marry younger. Besides as an income earner a woman's scale of expenditure would be lower. She'd have no time for the department store. Then too, spending would not be her only source of prestige. She would not be gauged by her circle on her scale of expenditure. 'What will become of beauty?' was launched against us by the same woman who had so poignantly let slip: 'I'm wondering what will become of the children?' Later in the evening I heard this

champion of aesthetics and of incessant maternity exclaim
to a male sympathizer, 'But I like pretty clothes.' 'Thank
God you do!' he rejoined....

The discussion closed with an exposition by a physician
of the latest theory of difference between the cells of male
and of female. Sound enough biology no doubt but quite
irrelevant to the subject, in view of our ignorance of the
relation which should exist between the cell and productive
labor, whether the cell be male or female or the labor that
which is now assigned to men or that which might be
assigned to women. But the irrelevancy was unnoted by
the anti-feminists present who as usual argued that society,
aware of the physical differences between the sexes, has put
men and women with unerring judgment into places
determined by those differences. In the name of society
how conceited we are about ourselves! Ignorant and
irrational creatures, we are ever putting forward our claims
to omniscience and rationality....

But the party was a success. The talk was not brilliant,
but there was talk (except by the few who on any such
occasion plan to keep their prestige by the exclusiveness of
silence), and the Anglo-Saxon self-consciousness was less
chilling and overcoming than usual. I hope there'll be
another party.

December.
Tonight at dinner they were full of last night's party. Two
of the women chimed in saying to me how much better off
in the discussion the college women appeared. They
themselves were not college women, but both their
daughters are to enter college in a year or so.... I collected
views on the way the women and men had been separated,
the women the speakers, the men for the most part the
listeners. Not a woman approved of it.... 'It made the talk
less brilliant...'. 'It would discourage the men from coming
to another party...'. 'I never serve on an organization in
which the women are put into a corner as an auxiliary
committee, why should I go to parties where the men sit in
a row actually and mentally behind the women...'. 'It just

emphasizes the tendency we now have in 'Society' for women to talk and men to listen. It's one of the reasons why our 'Society' is so dull.' All these were opinions from women. The one man I 'interviewed' liked the segregation. It was such a relief at a party not to have to pay attention to women as women, he said. Women's greed for men in polite society was so tiresome. No woman was comfortable, every man felt, unless she had a man talking to her.

Washington DC, December 6.
I've been talking or rather listening to Mrs F, who is particularly interested in the eugenic movement. The Yale University authorities have been considering, she tells me, the giving of a special performance of 'Damaged Goods' for the college students.[29] She herself would like to subsidize or partly subsidize a company to act the play in all the college towns of the country. Certain changes she would like to have made in the play to make it more effective for the American audience. The danger of infection for the wet-nurse has little or no bearing, she urges, in a country where, unlike France, the wetnurse hardly figures. I know of at least one case, however, where a trained nurse was infected by a syphilitic infant and became blind. Then the anguish caused a woman by gonorrheal, sterility-producing infection ought, she thinks, to count in the play. Furthermore two special appeals might be made by the play to the American man as an American. His characteristic kindness towards women might be appealed to, and his dislike of paying for a thing more than it is worth. If it is clearly put up to him, the American youth, untemperamental as he is, will be especially unwilling to indulge in 'indiscretions' at so great a price. This evening after dinner Mrs F was produced as a topic of conversation by the ladies. Quite evidently they disliked her. 'And how ridiculous she is about her eugenic society', said one. 'Yes, and all the more so because she has no children of her

---

[29] *Damaged Goods.* See note 10, above.

own.' I like Mrs F and so I spoke up: 'Oh, do you have to have children to be interested in children?'[n]

January, 1914.
We have had another discussion party – the last met the demand according to G. and H. of so many fair and fashionable ladies. The subject the men appointed was *chivalry*, and they held to it despite the query of one of the wranglers, 'why discuss a corpse?' The best we could do of course was to pretend to vitalize it – for a while at least. So I thought the chair made a strategic mistake when she held to having a definition and even asked the lady who had read a poem in praise of chivalry, her own poem, if she thought that a woman could be chivalrous to a man, an old man to a youth, a valet to his master. 'They might', answered the poetess in good Irish. The poetess and those who gathered to her support were all for extending the meaning of the term. 'Of course,' urged an opponent, 'if you mean by chivalry all the virtues, none will disagree with your contention that chivalry has a future.' This would have ended the discussion had we been logical and, as someone said afterwards, had we not presented the appearance of talkers at whom one looks through a pane of glass, so little did one mind meet another.... 'Chivalry has ever been the code of a caste,' I said, 'and it has had an unusually hardy life. Strong from its sense of inner superiority it has gracefully foregone the outward marks of caste, and so it resolutely survives plutocratic or democratic inversions. In our own plutocracy or nominal democracy it is especially cherished, for it enables a man to keep a sense of caste, of superiority, without any trouble to his conscience as a supporter of Republican institutions. Being

---

[n] You do, we all know, to have your interest taken seriously. Are not 'old maids' children' a favorite joke? In legislative debate on child labor laws the childless or celibate legislator rarely escapes ridicule. At Bartle Bay, New Guinea, an unmarried woman may not nurse a first-born child unless she gives it a present (Seligmann, p. 488, n.1.). To appear sensible and normal interest in children should be based on the sense of participation that comes from having children of one's own. *E.C.P.*

a gentleman or a lady is a salve to republicanism.' 'It's a
pity chivalry can't be a salve just now to feminism,'
someone suggested. 'Exactly, the really strategic feminist
ought to proclaim her devotion to chivalry.' '...But she
doesn't. She says it stands in the way of her freedom,'
came from the camp of the poetess. 'It does too',
challenged a Southern voice. 'When I was in Washington at
the suffrage hearings the Southern Senators said they would
as soon give a vote to rabbits as to women. How was that
for Southern chivalry? It's mere contempt for women!' and
the pretty Southern woman went on indignantly in words I
don't remember, her emotion too diverting. 'That's not my
idea of Southern chivalry', interrupted another Southern
woman. 'What is your idea, Mrs C?' asked the chair. 'Very
different, but I can't express it. You tell them, Charles', she
said, turning to her husband. But Charles declined to enter
the lists, whether from lack of chivalry or for some other
reason it did not appear. 'Chivalry is just a way of showing
off to women. And they'll always be wanting to show off
and there'll always be women to sympathize with them',
said a woman well known as an economist. 'Yes, there are
women who don't want everything for themselves',
sputtered the poetess. 'But in another sense,' the economist
went on, 'chivalry affects only a small class. There's not
much of it among working people.' Taking up her first
point, an Englishman, born of a house whose history led
directly to the age of chivalry, remarked that chivalry in
truth had been just a means like any other of capturing
women. 'It's an excellent way of keeping them in their
place', said another man. 'The more afraid men are of their
competition, the more they talk chivalry to them.' [30]

New York, January.
There's been talk of appointing – judge of the Children's
Court. She is a young lawyer and for two years she was a

[30] 'chivalry'. Compare with Parsons' statement on chivalry in *Fear and
Conventionality* (1914): 'the very protection you afford them [is] barrier
in itself against them. It keeps them most rigorously and most subtly in
their place' (p. 76).

truant officer. 'She's a splendid woman,' says Amos, 'but I
couldn't recommend her for that position.' 'Because of her
inexperience in the law?' 'No, that doesn't count for so
much in the Children's Court. But it needs a man. No
woman can manage adolescent boys. You must have been
a boy yourself to be able to influence a boy.'°

New York, January.
A man gave me a *résumé* last evening of the Fifteen Minute
Parent's talk he had recently had with his schoolboy son.
There had been a devil of a row in the boy's school. The
boy had been in no way implicated in the 'disclosures', but
he was considerably upset by them. 'There were three
courses open to a boy, I told him,' said the man, 'cold baths
and exercise, running with women, pervert habits. Pervert
habits played hell with your health and character,
undermined your courage; 'women' meant the risk of
horrible disease and gave you a sense of disillusionment for
the rest of your life, lessening if not taking away altogether
your chance of getting the very best thing life offers.'
'Physical discipline must be your recourse.... I know just
what you're up against. I went through it myself at your
age.' 'And,' the man went on to me, 'if my father had
talked that way to me, it would have helped a lot, for one
thing that makes it hard on a boy when this urgency of sex
is first upon him is the feeling that he is an exceptional
being, that in it all there is something peculiar to him...'.
There was no doubt in my mind that the man must have
helped his son – and, once the crisis was reached, more
than his mother could have done, or any woman.... But do
the Judges of the Children's Court help the boys who come
before them in any such ways?[31]

° Is that so, or is the view an expression of the same feeling of sex
solidarity which enforces the separation from women of tribal initiates?
E.C.P.
[31] 'must have helped his son...'. Parsons does not seem to question the
prescription of sexual abstinence the father offers his son. Despite her
ideal of 'trial marriage,' this entry makes clear that sexual relations
before marriage should, in her view, on the whole be discouraged.

January.
As we came out from the play last night onto the Broadway
pavement, a detective I know, a clever and quite charming
person, buttonholed Amos and after putting me in the
motor the two men went off together. They had a night of
it, as Amos, very sleepy, told me today. They had finally
after some months trapped their man, a husband who
would not agree to a divorce.[32] For a year he had been
living apart from his wife in an apartment. In it he
entertained his friends and they sometimes spent the night
with him. They were to do so last night. But a surprise
had been planned for them. The detective, Amos and the
wife went to supper together, in a little restaurant across
the street from the apartment. One of the detective's men
was in the street watching the windows of the apartment.
The surprise party was not to take place until the lights in
the front room, the sitting room, went out. It was a very
cold night and the man on the street joined the group inside
the restaurant from time to time for a cup of coffee. He
took six cups. The others drank coffee too and played
dominoes with the sugar. At about four am the lights
across the street went out and the whole party moved on
into the apartment house and, breaking down the door of
the apartment – it was chained – they went inside.... The
girl sat up in bed and called out, 'It's all right, I'm being
chaperoned.' She referred, they supposed, to the man and
girl in one of the other rooms. 'Did the wife go into the
bedroom too?' I asked. 'Yes, we thought she'd better.'
'...And this is what one has to go through to get a divorce
in the State of New York!' Amos said the detective would
exclaim to him from time to time over their coffee in the
restaurant. And yet the law is highly profitable – to
detectives.

January.
'Would you be willing to see marriage treated as an entirely
private affair in which the State has no voice?' I asked the

[32] Since the husband has refused his wife a divorce, Amos and the
detective have to establish the husband's 'unfaithfulness' before the wife
would be legally entitled to one.

three women after dinner last night. One woman was the wife of an ex-cabinet officer, one the wife of a physician, one the wife of a rich railroad man. (It really is difficult to place women as a rule except through men.) 'For myself, yes,' said [my downright hostess,] the doctor's wife, 'but I'm not sure about society.' And the answers of the other two amounted to the same thing. 'What is society? Isn't it I and you and you and you?' I began, and then the men came in, and conversation ceased and we formed a society of couples.... What is this 'society' that is always thrown at your head when you suggest a social change? Who is the other fellow for whom what is good for me is not good? And why is it not good for him? Is it because he is unknown to me, and whatever is unknown to me by a rooted habit of my mind I assume to be different from me with needs different from mine?

January.
Between us Herbert and I got a rather clearer insight into some of the perplexities of marriage last night as we ate oysters and drank beer in the little Sixth Avenue restaurant we frequent because it is quiet and because people go there who are more interested in one another than in others. Last night at supper there was a German card party of four in one corner, two men were playing a game of chess in another, and at one table some Frenchmen were forgetting for a moment they were not in Paris.... I had been telling Herbert the story of that early morning trapping, putting it in the form of a two act scenario, 'According to Law', I called it – scene one in the restaurant, the company drinking coffee and playing dominoes with the sugar, waiting for the lights across the street to go out; scene two, the breaking into the apartment with the girl in bed calling out that she was being chaperoned and the wife rejoicing in the idea of securing a million at least in alimony. But even with that extra melodramatic touch Herbert said at once that it wouldn't go, it was too trite, the public would not take in either the horrors of it, nor the satire. Catching a man like that was a commonplace. My scenario was a

mere photograph. I confessed that that was just what it was and then somehow or other we found ourselves talking of jealousy. The kind that goes with passion we both understood quite well, in fact, it was hard to conceive of passion without it, but the kind of jealousy that so often arises in passionless marriage was hard to understand at all. 'A man may be very fond of his wife,' said Herbert, 'he may like to do things with her, he may admire her immensely, their children and many other interests may be close ties between them and – that is all. But she won't have it that way. She insists on make-believe, altho' the passionate relationship means nothing in itself to her, probably has never meant much. But apparently no woman will give up the pretense of it.' 'Of course we know women are arch sentimentalists,' I rejoined, 'but I question your charge in one particular. Because a woman's passion does not show itself just like a man's, it doesn't mean it's not there. It's so much more distributed than a man's, so much more a matter of day in and day out, that a man may be blind to it. A wife's claim to monopoly may be really based on passion, not merely on vanity.' 'There may be something in that', he admitted.

The woman with whom Amos played that sunrise game of dominoes with the sugar, has been followed ever since by four detectives. For a time she went into hiding, never leaving her house. It is the second time her husband has set them on her. The first time was soon after she left him. She had taken a place as a bookkeeper; but she was so harried by the detectives that her employer was disquieted and she lost her job. There are, I recall, no children involved in this affair, and no money.... Approve ye, oh judges and medicine-men, of such persecution of one by another, even if the one is a wife and the other a husband?

The Stage Society gave an Elizabethan play yesterday, Thomas Heywood's *A Woman Killed with Kindness*. It was an extremely witty choice of a play. No modern problem play could possibly have presented the 'double standard' as grotesquely or the disaster of marital proprietorship as strikingly. Instead of killing her, the husband in his kindness banishes the erring wife to his untenanted manor, first putting her to shame before the children and the servants, *his* children and *his* servants. The lover, escaping the marital sword, but upbraided by his mistress as a fiend, looks forward to consolation in foreign parts and perchance in preferment at court. Meanwhile the repentant woman, vile strumpet, she calls herself, proceeds to starve herself to death, receiving on her death bed the pity of kin and neighbors and even the forgiveness of her husband.... I was so diverted that I read the play at home in the evening.

Could one get a more perfect bit of feminist propaganda by the ethnographic method? And yet the executive committee of the Stage Society, they tell me, is mostly anti-feminist.

January.
M. dined with me last night at the Colony Club. 'Don't the efforts of married people who are reduced to trying to get on together strike you as grotesque?' he asked after I had been telling him about the idea that has been circulating in my head for a parents' court. 'Grotesque enough for a mad house. But you lawyers don't generally seem to think so.' M. quite properly ignored my sarcasm and went on: 'As for the argument which lugs in the children, the stay-together-on-their-account theory, there's nothing in it to my mind if there's any friction at all between the parents. If they have an equable and pleasant *modus vivendi* it may be better for the children, I admit...'. 'Compulsory divorce at the end of every six years, is Herbert Walters' latest idea,' I laughed. 'Why six years?' 'Exactly, why six years?'

New York, January.
'Mother, do you believe in divorce?' asked Janet yesterday during the ten minutes we have together after lunch before she returns to school. 'I neither believe nor disbelieve. The important point is the relation itself between a man and a woman. If it is a poor relation, an unhappy or inadequate

relation they ought to end it. If it's a fine and happy relation they ought to continue it.' The child's mind ran away from the abstraction to the cases of divorce she had heard of in her family. 'I wish you would tell me the true story about Uncle Robert. I'm mixed up about it. Nobody will ever tell me what happened.' 'Part of it can't be told, because it's a private matter, a matter between two persons who first loved each other and then hated each other, and that we outsiders can't go into. I'll tell you the end of it though, a matter in which the public had to have a concern.' And I told her. It was a melodramatic story of the kidnapping of the children by one parent and their re-kidnapping by the other, ordinarily law-abiding persons assisting in each feat. 'Mother, it's like a game of chess', said Janet. 'In which one at least of the players was so unkind,' I added, 'that the sooner it came to an end, the better for all.'

In the evening I read my paper on the future of the family before the Cosmopolitan Club. It was a plea for the separation in theory of the two groups of facts, marriage or sex-relations in general, and parenthood, and it advanced a suggestion for a parents' registry and a parents' court in place of marriage bureaux and courts for matrimonial property and divorce laws.[33] Professor S. of Jena went into the history of the family to show that whether we liked it or not it was an institution subject to change. Professor R. of Columbia pointed out how hard we took change, fortifying ourselves against it with the arguments that it was contrary to human nature, to the will of deity, to the good of the other fellow. After us, two old-fashioned matrons spoke and two medicine-men. They all talked a good deal about the sanctities of the home and the blessings of conjugal love. 'If we have but the spiritual side of love,' declaimed one of the priests, 'all will go well. Of course if we have only the other side...'. That was good third century talk.... Professor R. remarked to me afterwards

[33] Parents' courts. These are Parsons' own proposals. See 'Marriage and Parenthood: A Distinction', *International Journal of Ethics*, 25 (1915): pp. 514–17.

that they were incredibly satisfactory exhibits. It was a very diverting alignment indeed of scientists and mysticists – economist, historian and ethnologist – arrayed against the pillars of society. A neater division I think I have never seen.

I spent part of yesterday afternoon at Wana-maker's. What a [diverting] social centre such a department store has become. It is a new institution or rather a *reconcentrado* of several old institutions. It aims to be all things to all men or rather to all women. It is a place for rest and recreation and assignation, market and fair, workshop and laboratory, social science seminar, hospital and nursery, and – *church*. Within a corded off space, hemmed in by eager-eyes women three rows deep, stood a bride and her bridesmaids. The bride carried a prayerbook and somewhere on an organ the Lohengrin wedding march was being played. An elderly woman next to me whispered quite as if we were standing side by side in a pew: 'She's a lovely bride, isn't she?' Only the priest and the bridegroom were missing – more or less.... Were you better social psychologists, oh you priests, better guardians of your dominions, you would rise up in wrath and denounce in horror from the pulpit such a mockery of your functions. A Wanamaker wedding is far more undermining to your sacrament than any aldermanic secularization or any discussion at a woman's club. Sometime the shopper, the female backbone of the city, may ask herself, 'what after all is a wedding but clothes...?'

Light on a more frankly economic subject also shone for me in that store. If the high cost of living is a real problem, [new subjects must be introduced into the curriculum of the schools.] Girls should be taught to resist the impulse to buy. Perhaps the teaching could be tacked on in the school curriculum as a kind of rider to the teaching of sex hygiene. From what I saw yesterday, the impulse to buy would seem to be more compelling, far more of a craving than the impulse of sex – at least with women of a certain age.... [Why shouldn't we have, by the way, a school for the middle-aged?]

I read my paper on the future of the family to Amos this afternoon. He had not heard it at the Club. He made two comments – one explicit, one implicit; first that the State would not make what I have called a parent's contract with anybody, it would only exert its police powers; second, that my whole plan was nonsense.... 'There must be marriage laws,' said Amos, 'lack of them would encourage loose living. A man who lives with a woman unmarried to her leads a merely sensual life. He has no sense of obligation.' 'You mean that the same man if married to the same woman would have a sense of obligation?' I asked, interested as usual in the mystical, legal ideas of Amos. 'The same man', he answered. 'Then he gets his sense of obligation, as you call it, merely through a ceremony? Can't two persons of themselves work out a system of mutual obligation? Even if they've gone through a wedding haven't they to do this in ways the marriage laws don't touch upon at all? If you were married and divorced and then lived again with your ex-wife without ceremony, would your relation be different from what it had been in legal marriage?' 'Yes, it would.' And then, an uncommon occurrence, Amos turned questioner. 'Wouldn't yours be in like case?' 'No,' I said, 'my relation to the one I loved would always have been determined by his personality. A ceremony wouldn't change his personality...'. We got on to divorce. 'Loose divorce laws keep people from making the best of each other,' said Amos. 'I wonder if 'making the best of each other' is really your conception of marriage', I queried. 'Why should people make the best of each other? You think people should marry for love and only for love?' 'Yes.' 'Is marriage a single act or a continuous performance? If they should be in love the first day, shouldn't they the second day, the third day, and so on? If ever they fall out of love shouldn't they cease to live with each other, once they are sure they are through?' 'There's no law now to keep people from separating. The law is that they may not marry again.' I made one more effort to get him away from the law to the facts. 'Being in love is an admirable experience, isn't it?' 'Yes.' 'Is it an experience that one may have only once in a lifetime?' 'No, but it must always be entered upon in the expectation that it will endure.' 'But that is the very nature of the experience. Passionate love is a treasure its possessor hopes never to lose. Married or unmarried one has that feeling about it...'. I do try to get at Amos' point of view – because I like him and because it is, I realize, in most particulars the collective point of view. But it is very elusive. By forcing the married 'to make the best of each other' by letting them have nothing else, does he mean that people may be starved into conjugality, half a loaf being better than no bread? But in other connections he does not describe conjugality as a merely physical appetite. It is very baffling. And again I ask why has loving to be justified by the attribute of permanence? The more 'spiritual' it is, the less physical. I even venture to suggest, the less enduring. Habits, particularly physical habits, endure; fancy, imagination, the sense of joy, are fleeting. Is love a habit or is it something else?

New York, January 27.
The Stage Society gave a 'problem play' yesterday, 'Heap Game Watch'. It was a poorly written play, but the point of it interested me, it was such a striking illustration of how the age class to whom sex no longer makes an appeal insists on governing the affairs of youth. In obedience to 'the inner law' a Montana cattleman ignores the game laws of the State. When he and his are hungry for meat he kills elk. He has a daughter who is in love with a forest ranger. The ranger was married at eighteen and after some years of conjugal nagging left his wife. He has not seen her for ten years. He has written to her asking her to get a divorce, but she won't, 'She's the kind of woman who won't let go'. Nevertheless the cattleman's daughter decides to go with the ranger. To her dismay she finds she has made a mistake in counting on her father's sympathy. In her case of hunger the inner law does not apply. So outraged in fact does her father feel by her design to ignore the laws of marriage that he resolves to keep the game laws and marches off to give himself up to justice, leaving the girl

bent but not broken by his vehemence.... I am moved to try another magazine with my paper on *Sex and the Elders*. It really is important, I believe, to get into the social consciousness the idea that the control of sex has always been in the hands of those free from its urgencies. It is indeed a government without representation, and of conditions far more significant for us than any condition politically determined. Isn't the time ripe for revolution, for an assembly of the rebels, beginning let us say with Catullus?:

> Vivamus, mea Lesbia, atque amemus,
> Rumoresque senum severiorum
> Omnes unius aestiveremus assis.[34]

New York, January.
'What did you really think of Professor S's address at the Cosmopolitan Club?' a man asked me last night at dinner. 'His dirge or elegy on the Family was ingenious enough to be amusing,' I answered, 'but his point of view was too exclusively economic to be convincing. Don't you think cohesive influence on the family is habit rather than any type of economy?' 'Why didn't you say that at the meeting? It would have been such a comfort to some of the old ladies and gentlemen sitting near me.' 'I fear I wasn't thinking very much about their peace of mind at the time,' I rejoined.... An incident that occurred after dinner showed how ruthless our Elders themselves can be – whenever they get a chance. Standing before the fire in a small group of women, I had made a reference to the *conversazione* of a few weeks past on chivalry. One of the women in the group was an elderly connection by marriage of the hostess on that occasion. 'I thought of going to that party', she said, and the bitter and cutting note in her low, thin voice caught the attention of all of us. 'If I'd gone I would have

---

[34] 'vivamus, mea Lesbia...'. The words of Gaius Valerius Catullus (84?–54? BC) to his mistress are translated by F.W. Cornish: 'let us live, my Lesbia, and love, and value at one farthing all the talk of crabbed old men.' Loeb Classical Library, London: Heinemann, 1966.

said just one thing – 'Ladies and gentlemen, you are all here in this house thanks to the chivalry of one man, the host who is not present." She did not have to explain her meaning. We all knew that a week or so after the party our hostess had applied for a divorce. We knew too that her husband's family, a large clannish family, were all set against her. But at that moment of denunciation last night I think I was the only one to recall that the venomous old lady had suffered in her own youth from the intolerance of the elders in *her* husband's family, an intolerance long passed away, for curiously enough we were dining that very night in the house of one of them, nevertheless an experience that might have made her more gentle towards the conjugal mishaps of others, had she been – younger. The old are hard and make life hard. Some day we shall cease to sentimentalize over them and keep them in the place they deserve. 'You mean you'd bury them alive like the – or, like the Eskimo, set them out in a snow bank?' I hear in outraged tones. 'Not so, I merely would not listen to them when they undertake to tell me what to do in matters they can no longer *feel*.'

January.
'I was talking today to one of our court attendants about your plan of doing away with marriage laws', remarked Judge – at teatime. 'What's that but free love? Haven't we enough of that already in New York', he exclaimed. Again the implication that but for law, every man would change his mate as he changes his shirt. Tired of one woman, he would take another – daily or at any rate every other day. Monogamy is a self-imposed bondage,[p] say the most zealous of its defenders; there can be nothing about it

---

[p] i.e., for the male. And it must be made worth while. 'If obey is to be left out of the marriage service to please the woman, the man may wish the words 'forsaking all others keep only unto her' also to be omitted.' And the Rev. E.J. Hardy adds: 'It is dangerous to play with a two-edged tool.' (*Still Happy Though Married*, p. 165. New York, 1914.) E.C.P.

instinctive or natural. Paul, Paul, do you never turn remorsefully in your sainted grave![35]

January.
'A man came into my office today, a literary man, to get me to straighten out a mess he's in with a woman.' — was walking home with me after seeing the Altman pictures. 'He had been living with her a year or more, first in her place and then in his. They broke off, and now she's after him for money. She has a child, not his, and she can't support it, she alleges, unless she goes back to her old profession.' 'Did he pay her at the time, night by night so to speak?' 'Yes, regularly that way at first; later he paid the rent of the apartment.' 'What does he owe her then – in money? It's just blackmail.' 'Of course it is, and she threatens exposure.' 'Is he married?' 'No, but he told her he was while living with her. She has found out he is a bachelor, and she may bring a breach of promise suit. He's awfully upset and he says he can't stand the publicity.' 'But there's no end to blackmail on that basis, once you yield.' 'I told him that...'. We dodged across the Avenue and turned into the street I live on, one of those depressing 'residential' New York streets hard to think of as leading to anybody's home. The chattel character of women is far from being lost. Are not the Literary Man, his ex-mistress, and the public he fears and she fools, are they not all ruled by the theory of the proprietorship of the male? In getting rid of marriage laws perhaps the law against 'a breach of promise' had better go first.

January.
How uneasy the women who would have been the most placid and self-satisfied anti-feminists a year or so ago! I talked with two of them today - one a white-haired,

[35] 'Paul...sainted grave'. Parsons refers to Saint Paul's authoritarian and sexist teachings on the subject of sexual relations. In particular, he enjoins wives, 'subject yourselves to your own husbands, as unto the Lord. For the husband is the head of the wife, even as Christ is the head of the church...' (Ephesians 5. 22–23.)

comfortable woman of sixty-five who said so defiantly that she stood for nothing but keeping her home and bringing up her family one was almost tempted into asking her what feminist creature she knew who wanted to invade her home or kidnap her children, the other a younger matron who got me into a corner and said, 'My dear – you know how fond I am of you; what *do* you think of feminists?' 'My dear Mrs P—, what do you think of dinosaurs?' I was pert enough to answer.... Pathetic ladies! In their inability to keep from talking suffrage or woman-in-the-home or what-is-to-become-of-the-children, they confess so plainly that they feel they are being washed up on the beach by a tide that they may never hope will launch them again.... My jibe did not succeed of course in turning the searcher after truth away from it to paleontology. 'Well, do you really think the vote would do women any good?' she went on. 'A little, but only a very, very little. It doesn't do men so very much good, does it? It's more important to women to get rid of their petticoats than to get a vote. And it's still more important for them to get a good job.' The reference to petticoats gave her a peg. 'Do you think then that women ought to dress like men?' 'It would be a pity in one way, wouldn't it, our men's clothes are so very ugly.' Just then the motor we were in reached the Metropolitan Museum. 'Goodbye, I am going in to look at the jades with a well dressed – Chinaman.' I suppose she didn't believe me.

New York, January.
I lunched yesterday at Claremont. The river was full of broken grey ice, but the sun was hot on the glass of the verandah. They won't let women smoke on that pleasant verandah on the theory, I supposed at first, that restaurants, like women, with no reputation to lose were most careful about them. But at tea time after a walk along the river we stopped in another park restaurant likewise dependent on the Board of Aldermen for the privilege of existing, and in it too I was told I might not smoke – unless I withdrew to one of the curtained off alcoves responsible, I suppose, for the character this restaurant bears as a place

'where ladies may not go'.[q] The New York Board of Aldermen does not believe in women smoking – whatever it may think of curtained-off alcoves.... I humored my own prejudice against alcoves until I quite forgot to feel cross [about them or that I wanted to smoke], so well entertained was I by the story told by my companion of another governmental valuation. Our New York Postmaster, it seems, has forbidden the use of the mails to a recent number of the *Cosmopolitan Magazine* because of a picture in it of Manship's bronze 'Centaur and Dryad'. Manship is a graduate of the American Academy of Rome, a young sculptor to whom Herbert Adams, President of the National Sculpture Society, has recently referred as 'a man who, if given a chance to work out his natural bent, may do American art an incalculable good'. Elsewhere in the same letter I am quoting Mr Adams mentions the 'Centaur and Dryad' as particularly distinguished among Manship's bronzes, adding: 'Have we in this country ever had such beautiful workmanship backed by artistic knowledge?' The Metropolitan Museum of Art has bought the 'Centaur and Dryad', and at the very time the New York Postmaster was suppressing the magazine containing a picture of it the Rockefeller Endowment Trustees, influenced by Mr Adams' letter and the account of the Academy in which it was incorporated, were voting a fund of $250,000 to the Academy of Rome. – What a comic people we are!

'I have a marginal disbelief in woman suffrage', said Professor B. at our Claremont lunch-party. 'I fear it would increase the great silent vote.' 'Temporarily, of course,' said some one, 'but isn't that disadvantage to be gauged by how far ahead you are willing to look?' 'Yes, of course', answered the Professor. 'When I taught at Barnard College I used to canvass my classes in woman suffrage. I canvassed at least ten classes. Always there was a heavy

---

[q] On questioning Cynthia about this interesting taboo, she gave me further details. One reason a lady is supposed not to go to this restaurant, she said, is because she might see there a man she knew with a disreputable woman. Of course he wouldn't look at the lady or bow to her under those circumstances but it 'might be awkward'. *E.C.P.*

negative vote.' 'I'm rather surprised by that,' I commented, 'In my day, the girls were indifferent.' 'Yes, but when it comes to a vote, the indifferent ones vote in the negative.' 'You wouldn't get a negative vote now of course.' 'No, but that's not due to the college women themselves; but to English militancy.'[36]

February.
I see in today's paper that Heflin of Alabama led the opposition in the Democratic caucus to the creation of a committee on woman suffrage by the House. The caucus voted 123 to 57 against the proposition.... Heflin is the Alabama Representative who was returned by his loyal constituents to Congress after wounding a white man in a Washington street car while he was shooting at a negro. His shooting up of the car happened while I lived in Washington and the story circulated at the time in Congressional circles was that although the Representative had been on his way to address a temperance meeting that evening he was not himself.... This is not the first rather curious juxtaposition of the rights of women and negroes in our country. Oberlin was the first college open to women and negroes. The Woman's Rights movement grew out of the anti-slavery movement, theoretically and practically.[r]

Washington DC. [Given.]
Last night at the dinner to [?given to] the Secretary of State I sat next to a Representative from Tennessee. He turned to the topic of woman suffrage just as in bygone days he

[r] Not so curious. The exclusive minded is exclusive towards sex and towards race alike. E.C.P.

[36] I have supplied what I assume to be missing quotation marks between 'vote in the negative' and 'You wouldn't get a negative vote now of course'. Thus I have assigned the words, 'You wouldn't get a negative vote now of course' to Cynthia, and the final speech dismissing the US college women's support for suffrage as attributable to 'English militancy' to Professor B. This reading seems to make more sense in terms of the characters' respective political positions, and the satirical thrust of the passage as a whole.

would have turned to the play running its week in town or to the flowers in the centre of the table, as a possible meeting ground with the woman next to him. 'The South has not been as much interested in woman suffrage as the North or West, particularly the West, but it's bound to come all over the country I think.' I looked across the table at Mr Bryan and thought that times had changed from the afternoon I had first met him in the White House. It was at a reception given to the Governors of the States by Mr Roosevelt. I had opened the subject of suffrage with Mr Bryan, who had promptly closed it with a plea not to bother him, and by telling one of those 'funny stories' American statesmen, ever evasive and gracious, could not get on without....

I suppose I broached suffrage to Mr Bryan as I did to many others that winter in an attempt to take the idea out for an airing. In those days – it was a year or two before the militant outbreak in England – it lived in the most unventilated and darkest of quarters, completely deprived of social life. The coming out party I planned for it was not much of a success.* I sent out cards, asking the recipients to subscribe themselves for or against it and if against it to give their reasons. I had few answers and never could I get started what was intended for an endless chain. Nowadays the anti-suffragists are quite as keen to give you their reasons as the suffragists.

---

*Nor, at a later period, was an attempt I made on presidential opinion. President Roosevelt had expressed pro-suffrage views when he was a member of the New York legislature and subsequently at Washington he had repeated them, but so lacking in his usual emphasis was this reiteration that it was construed by the editor of the periodical he was some years after to be associated with as anti-suffrage. Certain Massachusetts suffragists whom I knew wrote, asking me to urge the President to make a more emphatic declaration for suffrage in view of the publicity given the editor's misinterpretation. [The President answered the letter I wrote him as follows:][37]

> It was a pity Mrs D. [The — of the —] was not on the other side of the gentleman from Tennessee. I might have had some fun, and she might have turned the congressman into a really zealous suffragist. She is in Washington, and one of her last converts to suffrage I met at dinner tonight – a State Department man. 'Woman Suffrage!' Mrs D. had exclaimed to him last night at her son's dance, 'my dear boy , you don't know what it will lead to – socialism, anarchy, free love, and *that* is only a preliminary.' [During their talk there was some mention of Carrie Chapman Catt.[38] Mrs D's son overheard it and called out as he passed by: 'Oh dear, why did you let Mrs Catt out of the bag on mother?']

New York City.
On my way back from Washington I lunched in Baltimore. Our waiter said that ladies were allowed to smoke in the dining room. I only had a whiff or two, however, before the head waiter came up and said, not to me, but to the man at lunch with me, that it was not permitted. 'Perhaps next year you will allow it', I smiled, and perhaps next century, I added to myself, it will be good manners for men to communicate directly with women and not through other men, men now supposed to be responsible for them. 'Madame,' said the head waiter, 'if it depended on me you would smoke now; but what can you expect of a small town?' He was a Frenchman....

Professor H. of Yale came to tea today. A performance of 'Damaged Goods' has already been given at New Haven – 'quite unnecessarily,' said the Professor, 'the boys know all about that sort of thing.' Professor H. is giving a course

[37] I have been unable to ascertain what Roosevelt responded to Celia's letter. Tantalizingly, the manuscript leaves a gap at this point.

[38] Mrs Catt. Carrie Clinton Lane Chapman Catt (1859–1947) was the leader of the National American Woman Suffrage Association, the larger and more conservative of the two main US suffrage organizations. (The other was the National Woman's Party.)

in ethics and in it he included a lecture on the ethics of marriage. 'Why not have an entire course on that subject?' I asked him. 'You couldn't,' he answered, 'you can treat marriage only incidentally. It's too near home for the undergraduate.' Analogously, it was once improper to talk about religion or politics at the dinner table. What better evidence than these taboos of speech of the non-rational character of our institutions or at any rate of the adherence we give them?

February.
I went through the admirable laboratories of the Rockefeller Institute yesterday. No women were engaged in the research work, but in the preparation of material three women were employed, an older woman with two apprentices trained by her. I forgot to ask Dr F how the sexes came to be distributed in this way, the usual way.... Later in the afternoon one of professor G[idding]'s graduate students came in to see me. The subject of her university dissertation is feminism in socialistic theory. She wants to *organize* the woman movement in this country. We agreed that when suffrage passed out as a peg for feministic propaganda, a rallying cry, we should be at a loss. But the girl's desire to organize a thing as big and as imminent as feminism disconcerted me. Was it not better to leave it in the air, meeting one at every turn, everyone talking sense or nonsense about it? Did it make much difference which they talked as long as they talked? Indeed does not feministic theory bid fair to outrun practice? Is there not a danger of a shortage of women to do the things it is agreed upon they should be let do? But my caller was too much impressed by the actual lack of economic opportunities for the women who are seeking them to be impressed by this point of view or by my anti-organization attitude. Just then Amos came in. He was inclined to think that as many economic opportunities were open to women as they were as yet fit to take advantage of. 'Were you trying to earn your living as a professional woman, you might not think that', said the student, turning to Amos.

'Yes', said I, switching over to her side without much compunction. 'Take your own profession, Amos, the law. To begin with, you wouldn't be allowed to read law in the library of the New York Bar Association.' Amos laughed. 'She knows,' he explained to the student, 'for she was the first and as far as I know the last woman allowed to use that law library. It was when she was in college [compiling her doctor's dissertation on education in the American Colonies] and I had to get the permission for her...'.[39] With the exclusiveness of the Bar Association in mind together with a letter in this morning's *Times* protesting against excluding women from a civil service examination for city accountant, I have been writing to the Student urging her to give her organization the very definite goal of increasing opportunities to work for women. Let the country be raked through for its prejudices and discriminations against the employment of women *qua* women. Through a paid secretary and a *list* of influential persons let the attacks on the prejudiced and the discriminators be systematic and persistent. Let them be harried into self-defense.... If women are not eligible for reasons other than sex prejudice, new questions will arise to be faced, perhaps by educators, perhaps by parents, perhaps by employers. But first we must clear the field of the *débris* of sex prejudice....[s] Besides we ought to give a different bent to the direction of popular thinking on the employment of women. It is so obsessed just now by 'what-is-to-become-of-the-children' that it is shut to other considerations. I had an illustration of that last night at dinner. A young Harvard instructor sat next to me. It is the season of mid-year examinations and he had conceived the phantastic idea of correcting his examination books at the Knickerbocker

[s] As if you could! Cynthia, you *are* a *doctrinaire*, hide it as you will. E.C.P.

[39] The subject of Parsons' own PhD dissertation, completed in 1899 and published by Columbia University was *The Educational Legislation and Administration of the Colonies*. As Amos did for Cynthia, Herbert Parsons secured permission for Elsie to use the New York Bar Association Library.

Club. He knows, it seems, a well-to-do Boston woman who has turned her two young children over to someone to look after in order to take a lucrative job in an office in Chicago. So outraged did he feel over that situation that the idea of the employment of women who 'did not need to make a living' filled him with hostility. To considerations of age, of individual capacity or adaptation or inclination he was quite indifferent. Nurses, day nurseries, and boarding schools were anathema to him. Every woman should bring up her own children without assistance from any other person or agency. 'That would keep any woman busy.' 'It would', I said, and I asked him if he did not want to finish his cigar in the motor since he had not heard Farrar in *Tosca*.

February.
A talk yesterday with R.C. was enlightening. He had been reading Ellen Key,[40] and as we walked up and down in the one spot in New York possessed somewhat of the charm of the city where he had passed his youth, he was stirred to asking me questions. In asking them he revealed what I take to be the characteristic attitude on love and marriage of his class, the New York middle-aged man of business. Let me sum it up: As a rule a man is in love, really in love, only once in his life, when he marries. But that kind of thing, romantic love, does not last. After a woman has borne children she cannot be as attractive to a man as the first pretty face he sees around the corner. However he would not part with his wife for anything, and the pretty face or even the charming mind of the other woman he might tire of, he thinks, within a week. He is not going to fall in love with her; it would be too exhausting. He is a polygamous creature, he knows, but should he indulge his

---

[40] Ellen Key. Turn-of-century social thinker, author of works critical of contemporary feminist movements. In *The Century of the Child*, for instance, Key argues that 'the opinion held by the feminine advocates of woman's emancipation, in regard to the nature and aims of the everyday woman, does violence to the real nature of most women'. (See *The Century of the Child*, New York: Putnam's, 1909: p. 97.)

polygamous instinct he asks himself if it makes others unhappy? He must keep a rein on himself, a close watch. I couldn't face that point of view, just then at any rate, and so I side-tracked him to what we might both care for at the moment, the twilight of a city – the sense of isolation the terrace gave us, an island in the mad currents of the streets, and then the immediate contrast of the Renaissance terrace with the mid-Victorian plotting of the park beyond, those absurd circles and triangles I had skated about as a child and in whose 'best places' for a game of marbles or of prisoner's base I had that childish sense of satisfaction which no subsequent form of proprietorship gives.... But there you have it – passionate love, the complete relation, once and for all; then when it passes, as pass it must from the careless hands of the married, conjugal 'fidelity' and abnegation or, if he is 'unfaithful', a light o' love and the sense of unworthiness. And why? Because our Fathers said so and because a man would not make his wife unhappy. But is that the real explanation? How about his unwillingness to fall in love a second time because it would be so 'exhausting'? And what of his theory of passionate love as 'exhausting'?[t]

North Carolina, February 13.
Here I am for a long week-end quail shooting. After a day's tramp yesterday with a few scattered birds there are three or four inches of snow on the ground today and a driving and bitter cold sleet overhead. The men proposed rabbit shooting. I agreed to go until I overheard them planning to go out to the schoolhouse road in the motor. Then the grotesqueness of piling up to the day's trials of inclemency for a rabbit a motor, guns, dogs and men came over me and I gave the shooting party the slip and walked across country alone. I stopped in at a neighbor's to warm my feet. She'd had one daughter and seven sons, she told me; one son, a baby, died. 'You look pretty young to have had six children', she said. 'But you don't have to work.

---

[t]   It is a fairly common theory.

It's work which is breaking.' Broken she was indeed, with the set, cheerless look of the hard-driven farmer's wife. And yet there wasn't a line in her face, nor a grey hair on her head. [She was, I guess, about fifty.] Her fat, rubicund husband joined us, piling up the wood in the wide fireplace. Work had not broken him. His buoyancy was in striking contrast to the passive depression of his wife. Here in the clubhouse among the guests there is a somewhat analogous couple, howbeit from Philadelphia and of quite another economic class. He is still alive, but she is not. He remarked to me after our shooting yesterday that men were polygamists and women monogamists and that's where the trouble came in. 'For the woman won't face it, nor the man either, very often. How many *natural* men and women do you know?' he asked. 'Not a dozen, I bet.' 'If you mean that most of us are sentimentalists and try to feel the way we think we ought to feel, I'm with you.' He had no chance to tell me what he did mean, for we were interrupted. But he didn't have to tell me. When a man gets off that formula about the difference in mating between men and women, he at once classifies himself. He as much as tells you his wife is his easy chair and his mistress is the last 'pretty face around the corner'. [He knows passion and he probably knows love, but of passionate love he knows naught. There's nothing one can do for that kind of a man – except to keep him guessing. To any real relation he's not open.] That kind of a man is utterly at a loss how to classify you. He sees you smoke and he puts you in one class. He hears someone inquire about your children, the four or five of them, and he takes you out of that class and puts you in another. You tell him that with So-and-So you took a canoe trip last spring, and back you go into Class I. There you stay until he learns that you don't enjoy dining in restaurants and never take supper in a cabaret, and so into Class II with you. For him as with Weininger and the ancient Greeks there are only two classes of women, and into one or the other every woman he meets has to go. As a matter of fact the women he meets are unlikely to upset his classification as long as he continues to look at the world across the conjugal breakfast table of a morning and across the footlights of light opera of an evening.

February.
He is, it seems, a divorce lawyer or rather he has charge of the divorce cases which come into his office. 'I've seen so much unhappiness, I'd have divorce as easy as marriage,' he said to me last night, so this afternoon as we tramped through the snowy cornfields and the pine woods, he being bent on conversation I asked him why he did not try to have the New York divorce law changed, a law which makes people do such vile and ignominious things. 'They never will change it because of the Catholic Church.' 'But the Catholic Church doesn't control the State legislature. That's an up-State affair, and up-State New Yorkers are not Catholics.... At any rate why don't you try to get the breach of promise law off the statute book? The Catholic Church wouldn't make any objection to that.' 'Yes, we ought to get rid of that law; its only use is for blackmail.' Then we crossed a swampy 'branch' and became interested in pleasanter things than ecclesiastical influence or blackmail. The fine prints of the quail were on the thawing snow and a crowd of juncos were skipping through the briars ahead of us.

February.
He keeps referring to his wife as 'the head of the house'. It finally got so much on my nerves that I let out with: 'A man never calls his wife 'the head of his house' unless he knows she isn't, nor his 'better half' if he really thinks she is.' 'You're quite right'[u] spoke up his wife, a woman who will always be a naive, gentle little girl. 'I've never had a thing to say about the house.' He looked rather sheepish at me and retorted, 'you must be a suffragette...'.

---

[u] Also you're quite wrong, Cynthia. Such terms may be mere circumlocutions to avoid naming a wife – or a husband. (*The Old-Fashioned Woman*, pp. 177–9.) E.C.P.

New York, February 18.
I went last night to what its promoters advertised as the
'first feminist mass meeting'. The woman question or
women's rights we have had with us for some time, a
hundred years or so, but feminism, it seems, is quite new.
What a curious effect a new tag may have! Perhaps
'women's rights' was merely a new tag in its day....ᵛ The
meeting was in Cooper Union. I went expectant of
heckling; but while I was there there was none. The hall
was filled, and with the usual miscellaneous Cooper Union
audience, perhaps with a larger proportion of women than
usual. There was a scattering of Bowery loungers, but it
was on the whole a closely attentive, responsive audience.
The most decided applause was given to various statements
to the effect that our idle, parasitical women were our
greatest menace. A class war between women *is* no doubt
in the order of things. It may be a surprising kind of
ferment to the class war at large. At any rate last night
hints of it were unmistakable, whereas of sex-antagonism
there was little or no suggestion. That was probably the
reason there was no heckling. How far removed we were
from a kind of heckling once invariably a feature of an
open meeting for women's rights was evidenced by the way
the audience took to a story told by Frances Perkins.⁴² She
became, she said, a feminist at the age of eight. Brought up
in a community of boys, she was in every way like one of
them until the time came to lengthen her skirt. Then she
found out that when it came to belly whoppers or climbing
trees she was distinctly handicapped. So she borrowed

ᵛ Certainly. Consider only the titles of certain books of an earlier period –
*La Nobiltà e la Eccelenza delle Donne, con Defetti e Mencamenti degli
Uomini*, written by Lucrezia Marinella in 1602; *Dissertatio de Ingenii
Mulieribus ad Doctrinam et Meliores Liberas Aptitudine*, written by
Anna Maria Schurman in 1645.⁴¹

⁴¹ '*La Nobiltà...*'. 'The Nobility and Excellence of Ladies, and the Faults
and Deceits of Men;' 'Discourse on Women's Superior Aptitude for
Learning.'

⁴² Frances Perkins (1882–1965), social reformer. First woman US cabinet
member, as Secretary of Labor in the administration of Franklin D.
Roosevelt.

some 'pants' from a next door neighbor. It was a disastrous experiment. The boys refused to play with her; she was sent home from school; her father whom she had loved utterly oblivious of any difference between him and her in age or sex, her beloved father threw back his head and laughed at her. At the end of five days she slunk back into her petticoats and thereafter most of her recreation she spent in reading. 'She's one of those children who loves reading', her father came to say of her. The quick witted audience got her point and laughed, and I thought as I listened how seventy years ago the moment a woman stood up to speak on a public platform she was asked, 'Why don't you wear pants...?' Good as most of the speaking was, we did not escape a questionable aphorism or two. We had to hear, of course, that a people was to be gauged by the position of its women, witness beharemed Turkey, the most backward country of Europe, and the anti-suffragist South, the most backward part of the United States. One suspects an aphorism because, I suppose, it's so tiresome; but this particular one, or rather the pet illustration to it, took on fresh color for me as I read the morning paper. It gives an account of a debate over the etiquette of calling just held in the Congressional Club, a club that originated a few years ago at our Washington dinner table. 'Calling' in Washington as elsewhere is a form of impersonal companionship, a kind of merit-acquiring ceremonial. Its particular hold upon the unemployed of Washington is due to the illusion the women cherish that it is of advantage to their political husbands.[w] And so it may be, if not quite in the way the women think. 'Calling keeps women out of mischief,' I once heard a man say, 'but I'm damned if I can see why they do it.' There is in Washington a particular variety of the parasite woman the Cooper Union speakers abused, the political wife or 'young lady' daughter; but even they fret somewhat over their inactivity and so they find what they call their 'social duties' or paying from one to several dozen 'calls' each afternoon helpful to their self-esteem. When I

[w] He had not read Chapter X of *Fear and Conventionality*. E.C.P.

lived in Washington, the Southern women I found were
particularly tenacious of the right to pay calls, and it is
they, I surmise, who in this recent discussion in the
Congressional Club made the bulk of the winning vote in
favor of maintaining the time-honored practice. The
Southern pleader for woman-in-the-home would naturally
abet the ceremonial of calling, for if she is not to be in her
own home, let her by all means be in the home of some one
else. Nor as long as she is in a home does it matter particularly what took her to it or what keeps her in it.

New York, February.
As a member of the Committee of the Association of
Collegiate Alumnae I had an informal talk today with a
trustee of the American Academy in Rome. The Academy
does not admit women, not, according to its trustee,
because of any prejudice against them, but because of a
lack of room for them. They would of course have to live
in a separate building, said the trustee, and funds for one
are not available. 'Why a separate building?' I asked.
'Because of the proprieties.' 'Don't you realize that no
matter how urgent a love affair might become between the
men and girl Fellows, such would be their *esprit du corps*,
their professional sense, their feeling about their work,
whatever you like to call it, that their common building
would be the last place where the proprieties would fail to
be observed. A man never in the university world held a
girl's hand under the seminar table.' 'Well, in such a
scandal-mongering community as Rome it wouldn't look
well to have men and women students living in the same
building.' 'Where are the women students in the School of
Classical Studies to live?' (This School has just
amalgamated with the Academy and its men students are to
live in the Academy building.) 'In *pensions*, I suppose.'
'And so you American men say to American girls, 'Fend for
yourselves', in a city where a girl on her own, I have heard
you say, is fair prey. You're safer in a Roman *pension*, you
say to them, than in a group of your own countrymen. At
any rate *their* virtue and *their* good name have to be

safeguarded against you. What a striking illustration of
American chivalry!' The trustee is by no means a man slow
in retort, but to this sally he had nothing to say. 'At least
why don't you admit women to the fine arts division of the
Academy without the privilege of residence?' I went on.
'Because the greatest benefit coming to our Fellows is from
residence. It is the life together and with their Director that
counts. It's a question of atmosphere. The Academy
couldn't do its best for a student out of residence.' 'In an
Academy building, separate from the men, wouldn't
women students be somewhat non-resident, so to speak,
deprived of the stimulating atmosphere you mention...?' It
was an interesting discussion – to me at least. The contem-
poraneous state of mind of the fairly liberal professional
man towards the intrusion of women into his calling was
made so transparent. As bent on excluding them as was his
grandfather, he no longer appeals to Nature or St Paul; he
urges a lack of money or of floor space. He even makes of
Mrs Grundy a foreigner[x] the better to avoid any responsibility for her.[43] The sanctions or reasons change; but anti-
feminism is ever the same state of mind – 'We don't want to
have women around; we don't want to be bothered by
them.'

February.
The much talked of Venetian ball of the Fine Arts took
place last night. I dined before it at an antique table where
Byzantine ladies, Florentines and Venetians, a court jester,
a doge, and a cardinal looked strangely in place. Next to
me sat a Knight Templar *en route*, said he, to the Holy
Land. Meanwhile we talked of a crusade nearer home.

---

[x] Rather a mythological personage. The French Academy in Rome
admits women students on exactly the same terms as men. And Mrs
Grundy has had nothing to say. This spring I happened to lunch one
day in Rome with the Director of the School of Fine Arts of the
American Academy, and lunching with us was one of the women
students of the French Academy, also some of the men of the American
Academy. There seemed to be nothing dangerous in the situation.
E.C.P.

[43] Mrs Grundy. Proverbial typical prudish censor of public morals.

'Not one but twenty cases a day I have again and again,' he
said (in daily life he is a physician) 'of women who come to
me as they say in trouble. They are unmarried and
married. Often it seems certain to me that it's no fault of
theirs. But what in heaven's name can I do for them? I'm
not a gynecologist. I'm not a reformer. I'm interested only
in the human side of it all. And that is horrible. There's no
one I can send the women to. 'I can't touch that, it would
make me a social outcast,' every reputable doctor tells you.
The woman goes to a midwife. She becomes infected. She
goes to the hospital and in most cases she dies. The
hospital wards are full of such women, women dying
because in many instances they are unwilling to have
another child for the sake of the children they already
have... I'm more interested in these married women than in
the unmarried.' 'You may be,' I rejoined, 'and the public
may have to get interested in their plight first; but
eventually we shall all believe that no woman, married or
unmarried, should have to bear a child *against her will*....
Why don't you find a man more interested in the humanitarian side of gynecology than in the professional who
would be willing to curette [without furtiveness] any
woman who goes to him?' 'We had such a man six or
seven years ago, Conrad, and they jailed him for two
years.... How many women of your class could you find
willing to back up that sort of a stand?' 'Very many would
be in sympathy with it; but few would publicly declare
themselves – at the start at any rate. People are so extraor-
dinarily afraid of the subject.' [After a little address I made
the other night at the Cosmopolitan Club on the future of
the family, several persons in the audience complimented
me on my courage, as they put it. I don't know what they
had in mind unless it was my reference to the social
recognition of regulating conception...] 'But it is you
doctors who are most to blame. You take no social responsibility at all in this matter.' [And I told him in illustration
the story of the head gardener's wife.] 'As for curetting, it
is, you know very well, the crassest of class discriminations.

Any wealthy woman can get it done, and, as you tell me, no poor woman.' 'Yes, it is gross hypocrisy and injustice.'

This morning I wrote to Dr— suggesting that he write the story of the unwilling mothers for a recently published periodical in which all the articles are anonymous – for our first gun. Then let him inspire a gynecologist for the undertaking, turning over to me the task of collecting a group of women and men to back his man when the emergency arises, as arise it must.[44] Legislative reform will follow. Of course we should at once arm ourselves with statistics from the hospitals. The magnitude of the evil is certainly not generally realized.

He answered that he thought some representative medical society should take the matter up in a body, the American Medical Association or the State of New York Society. Of course he is right; but when will they do it?

February.

My Philadelphia-North Carolina acquaintance turned up yesterday at Lucy's, 'to be educated', he alleged. He was given opportunities. Alice and Frances[45] were there and they generously met his anti-suffrage tirades, becoming more and more gentle and patient the more the lawyer from Philadelphia was bewildered and evasive and irrelevant. 'Why take on the burden of voting?' he urged. 'I know a Republican officeholder in Philadelphia and to keep in the swim for years he has had to go to his political club every night. Why ask that of a woman...? Then by voting she will lose her feminine charm,[y] a woman's most

---

[44] The stand on abortion Cynthia proposes was very much that taken by Margaret Sanger on the teaching of birth control techniques in her New York clinic. When she was prosecuted for this activity, the response of Greenwich Village activists and intellectuals, Parsons among them, was, indeed, to 'back' her.

[45] Probably Alice Duer Miller and Frances Perkins (see notes 22 and 42, above).

---

[y] Other circumstances besides voting have been held to detract from the charm of one sex for the other. Among the Koita of New Guinea certain fish are not eaten by young people because it would make their

precious possession. It isn't in a woman's nature to vote.'
And so he went on. 'I believe, mind you, in the emancipation of women. I'd open all doors to them but that of
the ballot booth.' 'Would you,' I asked to relieve the
others, 'would you admit women to the law school of
Columbia or Harvard?' 'Of course not,' he answered
unabashed. 'I've had to practise against a woman lawyer
and I hated it. I'd get out of it whenever I could. So would
any other lawyer. I'd run away from a woman lawyer just
as I would from a woman who raised a cane against me in
the street.'

February.
'He's not jeering', said one of my guests last night, a lawyer
of another, Herbert Walters. Herbert had just remarked
that he did not see how a woman could be a surgeon and a
mother at the same time. 'He's not jeering. In spite of what
he says he's the only doctor I know who isn't at heart
against women coming into the profession.' 'Yes, I suppose
you lawyers are really less exclusive than the doctors. Why
is that, do you suppose?' It was the doctor who answered:
'Because there's more competition in surgery than in law.
There aren't enough people to cut up for the surgeons.
That's why they are against letting women in. That's why
a woman surgeon couldn't take enough time off to have a
child. She'd have to drop out. If a man surgeon were laid
up for eight months he'd have to drop out too.' One more
illustration of how the economic position of woman is tied
up with the economic organization at large, of how
thwarting to her must be organization based on
competition.
[And truly it is a man made society. Think only of the
surgeon who with one side of his mouth tells a woman that

---

skin harsh and render them unattractive to the opposite sex. In another
tribe wallaby is not eaten to avoid a like risk. In still another New
Guinea tribe it is believed that were men to eat fish of certain varieties
they would lose their charm for women and be denied feminine
favors. (Seligmann, C.G., *The Melanesians of New Guinea* pp. 139,
550, 681, n.1, Cambridge, 1910.) *E.C.P.*

she may not have a child and with the other side of his
mouth that she can't escape having a child.]

March.
'I'm late,' said Amos, arriving after tea-time, 'I had to hold
court in the office. Row among the stenographers. Our
managing clerk told me that Miss A, the senior stenog-
rapher, had said to him that unless he reported Miss B, one
of the junior stenographers, to me, she, Miss A, would.
They don't like Miss B's ways. She's flirtatious, they say,
and last night she didn't go home. Her mother telephoned
Miss A to ask her if she knew where her daughter was. She
had threatened before to leave home.' 'What did you do
about it?' 'Oh, I called in Miss B and told her she mustn't
leave home, if she wanted to keep her job.' 'How old is
she?' 'Twenty five or so.' 'Did you ask her where she was
last night?' 'Yes, with a friend in Hoboken, she said.'
   'Did you ever ask your managing clerk where he had
been that night last winter you needed him so particularly
and couldn't get hold of him until 6 am?' 'Of course not.
It's none of my business where he spends his nights...'
How insidiously 'the double standard' can work. No
doubt each of the four persons who were operating it
against Miss B yesterday would deny that she or he
believed in it – her mother, her fellow clerk, her superior
clerk, her employer. No, perhaps her mother wouldn't deny
it.

March.
An old-fashioned woman was among us last night. She
smoked a cigarette, to be sure, and she told the rest of us
women after dinner that the only reason she did not walk
in the suffrage parade was a lame foot. Nevertheless, she
was unmistakably old-fashioned.... [Her children were her
line of least resistance and she followed it.] The lame foot,
we heard, came from a knock in the dark one night when
she got up in a hurry thinking she heard a child cry. Had
she seen the Morgan collection? 'No, you know my baby
has been ill almost all winter.' The other two women
talked of Galsworthy's last novel. 'What is the name of it?'

she asked. 'I've had to read aloud so much to the children that my eyes have given out for my own reading.' It was to be Europe this spring for one of us. 'How I wish I could go; but of course I can't leave the children.' Portugal was mentioned. 'My young daughter asked me today what had become of the King of Portugal. Don't you think that was quite a remarkable question for a child of ten?' I asked Amos what she had talked to him about at dinner. 'She had a good deal to say about her house.... At first she didn't recognize me. She said it was because she hadn't seen me for so long. She'd been in quarantine with her children with the measles.... She's an awfully tiresome woman.' 'But as a rule, Amos, you admire the home-staying, devoted mother, don't you?' It was low of me, I confess.

New York, March.
'What *is* feminism?' asked of me a woman who has known me for a long time,[46] 'do tell me.' 'I have been telling you all my life'. I answered. 'When I would play with the little boys in Bryant Park although you said it was rough and unladylike, that was feminism. When I took off my veil or gloves whenever your back was turned or when I stayed in my room for two days rather than put on stays, that was feminism. When I got out of paying calls to go riding or sailing, that was feminism. When I would go to college, in spite of all your protests, that was feminism. When I kept to regular hours of work in spite of protests that I was 'selfish', that was feminism. When I had a baby when I wanted one, in spite of protests that I was not selfish enough, that was feminism.' 'All the same,' rejoined the lady with a laugh, 'you haven't answered my question. What you say only shows you've always been a rebellious daughter, nothing more than that.' The following day the lady sent Janet the white kid gloves and the gauze veil that Janet had asked her for – 'because Mother won't buy them for me'. I suppose our colloquy had reminded her of the request.

[46] 'a woman...'. This conversation is based on one which took place between Parsons and her mother.

New York, March.

'I'd like your opinion on a situation I'm mixed up in', said Herbert Walters last night as we were walking uptown through the Park. 'Three years ago I performed a major operation on a girl who from the life she'd been leading was in a very bad way. She convalesced, left the hospital, her friend paid the bill and that was the last of her – until yesterday. Yesterday she came in to see me – an entirely different looking woman, full of health and respectability. She's engaged to be married and she wants me to have a talk with the man. She knows she can't have a child. She wants me to tell him. I can tell him too that otherwise she is a perfectly healthy woman. The question is, ought I to tell him anything else? Ought she not to have this chance to pull out?' He was asking my opinion on this simple situation I supposed somewhat as a form of conversation, but I answered, 'Of course he ought to know about the inability to bear a child; but the rest of the story is hers to tell, not yours. And doesn't it depend upon the kind of man he is whether she'd do well to tell him or not? At any rate it's not up to you.' 'I agree with you', said Herbert.

March.

Miss P, bent on organizing, has organized a Woman's Forum in Columbia, a mistake, I think, seeing that the University or parts of it, stands for an identity of interests for the students of both sexes. The Forum had its opening meeting last night and I went, sacrificing the first two acts of 'Boris Gudunoff'. The general drift of the speakers, professors and graduate students, was the relation of the women's movement to democracy at large and the need, the immediate need of equal opportunity for women in our economy, or rather, as I come to think of it, of special opportunities, for all made much of Prof. Robinson's point that the crying need at present was a supply of half jobs for women. 'Half jobs', that is an unfortunate term, and catchy enough to take at large just as it did last night. If I had not been in a slow-witted mood I would have suggested a substitute. 'Half day' is what Prof. Robinson meant or, better still, piece work. 'Half job' carries a

sinister suggestion of amateurishness and incompetency.
[I'll write to R—. Miss P has the gift of the demagogue.
Within ten years she will be, I predict, a notorious woman.]

March.
'I once wanted to put a girl into my drafting-room,' said a
man I was lunching with today, ['she was clever and I
thought it would be a good thing to do'.] But I found the
men didn't like the idea at all. I called together two or
three of them to talk it over. 'You're not the kind of men,'
I said to them, 'who tell smutty stories. You're gentlemen.
I wouldn't have you in my office if you weren't.' What
difference did it make whether a woman worked with them
or not?' 'What did they say to that?' I asked. 'Nothing at
all coherent; but their feeling seemed strong. They were
really disquieted.' 'Probably because they had acquired it
at a very early age – from their mothers. Anti-feminism,
like so many other things, begins in the nursery. It's quite
true that a man gets his idea of women from his mother. I
suppose that girl lost her chance.' 'Oh yes, there wasn't
any use in upsetting the men so much.'

New York, March.
The dean of one of the leading women's colleges had a talk
today with the same trustee of the American Academy at
Rome, with whom I conferred a month ago. It was of
course about the exclusion of women from the Academy's
School of Fine Arts. 'Why wait until you have a separate
building for women?' The trustee was asked, he tells me,
by the Dean. 'Isn't it better to have them in the same
building with the men at any rate?' And then the Trustee
reiterated the reasons which he had already given me
militating against this plan – Roman gossip, the conservatism of the trustees of the Academy (to many of them, he
said, any feminist argument was mere unintelligible jargon
– it was not that they did not want to understand it, they
could not understand it) and last of all, and this point was
freshly emphasized by him, the opposition of the men
students themselves – they would not like to have women

students in their building. How the Dean met the latter points I did not hear; but with Mrs Grundy, Roman or American, she dealt summarily. 'Suppose there is an occasional flirtation, suppose in every twenty years or so there is even an unfortunate *liaison*, what of it?' What a significant retort! It means, does it not, coming from that respectable collegiate mouth that the chastity club is becoming a hollow reed, a pipe to play on perhaps but no longer a weapon of coercive terror?

Bully for you, Dean J...! As for those conservative trustees, their colleague told the Dean that the only pressure they would recognize would be finding themselves face to face with a clamorous group of well qualified women painters, sculptors, architects:

'Mother, may I go out to swim?'
'Yes, my darling daughter;
Hang your clothes on a hickory bush
But don't go near the water!'

That women have never distinguished themselves in the arts is a not uncommon argument against their capacity, 'for surely in following the arts they have never been handicapped'. This passing controversy over their admission to the Academy at Rome makes one question that assertion. Have women always been freely admitted to other schools of art or to apprenticeship upon works of art? Did the artisan-artist guilds admit women? At what dates would a woman artist have been commissioned to decorate a public building? I wonder if this notion that women have had a free scope in the arts is not due to a misunderstanding of the arts themselves, to ignorance of their ritualistic origins and conditions, to oversight of the apprenticeship they demand, in short to an amateurish or dilettante notion of the nature of art? Is it not possible that art true to its origin in priestcraft has been preeminently exclusive of women, and that the 'conservative' trustees of the Academy at Rome are but loyal descendants of the Fathers, Early Century and Puritan...? As for the men students in the Academy, no doubt they *will* object to the presence of women. X. who was listening with me to the trustee's comment that of course the men would mind said that when he himself went to a restaurant for lunch he always chose a table where only men were sitting.^z It *is* a difficult alternative for the men students and for their guardians: aversion on the one hand, flirtation with them on the other. Your Scylla and Charybdis are trying, but oh Sirs, Fellows of the Academy, Director, and Trustees, what if you were to consider the women students first as students and then as women, would you have to go through the narrow waters at all?

New York, April.
The Woman's Forum in Columbia has happily changed its name to Feminist Forum, and, as it appeared last night, doubled its membership. Dr R[iddle] of the Carnegie Laboratory, Cold Spring Harbor, lectured on their research work in sex which indicates a quantitative and reversible basis of sex. His concluding remarks might readily be turned into anti-feminist argument. 'With conduct in conformity with our moral code, with late marriage, with the sexes mingling socially in shops and business, in education and the professions without sex stimulus, we have all the conditions conducive to a weak sex development for both males and females.' It might be said, of course, that our present code of morals demands a weak sex development and while it remains as it is people are happier and better off leading a comparatively sexless life…. Dr R[iddle] might also be asked a question or two about the distribution of the sex impulse. Among the non-human species failure to copulate may result merely in suppression of the sex secretions and consequent loss of sex characters, but in our species where sex impulse may be

---

^z Among us the feeling against eating with women expresses itself but erratically as in this instance or in the giving of 'stag' dinners or 'bachelor' suppers. But in many places there is a rigid taboo on commensality with the opposite sex. There is an island among the New Hebrides where a man runs the risk of a mysterious death by eating with a woman, and a Hawaiian woman who pushed her way into the men's eating room was killed. *E.C.P.*

directed to handicraft, art or science, to work with any constructive or inventive or dominating quality, may not the sexual secretions continue unabated or in fact more stimulated than through periodic copulation? Why do you think too, Dr R[iddle], that companionship between the sexes does not result in stimulation even if it does not lead to copulation? Among the non-human species and in that species among savages there is no sex stimulus between individuals of opposite sex but copulation or relations which if they are not consummated in coition bring disaster. In the modern companionship of the sexes may there not be in many cases a sex stimulus which does not necessarily lead to coition? Else how account for the romance of sex or for romantic love itself?

But the lecture suggested other points of an even graver and farther reaching significance than the merit or demerit of co-education or suffrage or work side by side with the other sex. It is suggested that sex is not an [in]eradicable, immutable character in any given individual. How much this fact may mean! When we are willing to meet it, how much it may change the face of our society! The day may come when the individual may be free to express sex, its sex, let us say, when it wishes to, when sex is really there to be expressed; but when sex is absent it does not have to be assumed, pretended to. Very little expression of it will be there prior to adolescence, very little again in the latter part of life. But even during that part of life which is highly charged with sex, it may be treated as the impulse it is, varying in quantity, sometimes lacking altogether. Nor will any individual have to pretend to be possessed of a given quota of femaleness or of maleness. There will be no common measure. This morning perhaps I may feel like a male; let me act like one. This afternoon I may feel like a female; let me act like one. At midday or at midnight I may feel sexless; let me therefore act sexlessly. Even nowadays women resent having always to act like women, or to be treated invariably as women. We think it is because they consider the position of women inferior. With many rebellious women no doubt that is all that is back of their resentment, but with some of the rebels, I surmise, mingling with that particular resentment is the desire for greater elasticity for their personality. It is such a confounded bore to have to act one part endlessly. Men do not resent being treated always as men because, in the first place, of the prestige of being a man and because, in the second place, they are not treated always as men. And yet men too may rebel some time against the attribute of maleness, applied even to the extent it is today. The taboo on a man acting like a woman has ever been even stronger than the taboo on a woman acting like a man. Men who question it are ridiculed as effeminate or damned as perverts. But I know men who are neither 'effeminate' nor pervert[47] who feel the woman nature in them and are more or less tried by having to suppress it. Some day there may be a 'masculism' movement to allow men to act 'like women'.

New York.
'Have you ever been really lonely?' asked Herbert Walters. 'I mean the kind of loneliness that amounts to acute physical distress.' 'I see so many lonely women,' he went on, 'and I hear of more. Girls who've come to New York and have no 'social connections' whatsoever. They've a job, but after their work is over there's nothing for them to do, and no place but their hall bedroom to go to. They haven't money enough to buy amusement – beyond the ten cent magazine. There's only one way for them to get the amusements they see around them. For six months or a year they stick it out; but after that I doubt if few of them return evening after evening to the utter loneliness and dreariness of their hall bedroom. What are you going to do about them?' 'Give them meeting places,' I answered, 'real *rendez-vous*. That's what we'll all come to. Why in the world should we go to 'shows', 'parties', 'functions', 'be entertained', 'invited out', submit to all kinds of indignities,

---

[47] Parsons' use here of such terms as 'pervert' and 'effeminate' – even to argue that men whose personalities contain a 'feminine' element are neither – does suggest strict limits to her acceptance of diversity in sexual orientation.

'descend to meet', or else be miserable in the lonely hall bedroom each of us keeps somewhere, when all that we want is companionship, an hour or two with someone with charm for us or with a group of gay or interesting persons. Backgrounds for such companionship, attractive meeting places, 'social centres', places for social reunion or adventure, are what we are to have – some day.' 'Some day perhaps,' Herbert smiled. 'Today there are no such places.' 'There's Lucy's.' 'Yes, there's Lucy's – for a few of you, a precious few.'

March.
Herbert had smiled incredulously over my panacea of common meeting places as antidote for the curse of loneliness and as to Lucy's tea parties[aa] furnishing the key to more than a stray handful he had been altogether scornful. But his incredulity and his scornfulness were an attitude, not an argument, so I was left merely wondering a little why what was so appealing to me was not to him. But I ceased wondering when I read a letter to The *Times* printed under the headline 'a lonely cry'. It is written by a woman writer on the staff of a magazine and is the story of her first months of loneliness after her arrival in New York. She was fitted, she writes, 'both by birth and education for a position in a clever and intellectual, though not necessarily a society, world.' 'My life,' she adds, 'had been devoted to books.... They were practically all I know.' In other words she had not been educated for life. Her phrase 'society world' still more betrays her; it is quite apparent that in her mind social life is rigidly divided into compartments. Further on in the letter, the conception of society as a matter of demarcation again crops out. 'I could not go out alone at night.[*] I had not been brought

* A restriction recognized by women in many places. (Unfinished.)

[aa] Cynthia's friend Lucy is a vagabond and when she is tramping she gives Cynthia and her set the use of her charming New York apartment. Fond as they all are of Lucy they say she is at her best as an invisible hostess, and that their one regret is she can't be one of her own guests. *E.C.P.*

up to do so, and custom and tradition live strong in me.
Besides, even if I went out, where could I go? I could walk
the streets – yes – but women – 'nice women' – do not walk
the streets of New York alone, even between seven and
eight o'clock in the evening.** I could not afford orchestra
seats in the theatre, and I shrank from the thought of the
gallery. I could not sit in the parks, even in the stifling
weather...'. Would there be the slightest use in providing
backgrounds for social adventure for this letter writer? A
'Society' world is really the only world she wants, a world
of set entertainments, of gregariousness without fellowship,
where everyone holds a well-recognized place, where
conventional openings are undisputed, and civilities are
encouraged, a world as devoid as possible of personal
relationships or of the chances of making them.... When
after four months of 'literally' never speaking 'to a soul
except the servants', our letter writer did attempt to enter
into a personal relationship and moved from her Madison
Avenue boarding house to an apartment on Morningside
Heights, a joint tenant with an 'acquaintance', what
happened? She had not been there a week before she found
that her 'acquaintance had ideas about making and
entertaining acquaintances that didn't at all correspond'
with hers. 'In fact when she suggested asking up a man or
two, and letting them bring up a beefsteak which she was
to cook in first-class style, I didn't see it that way. I
declined to be a party to any such transaction, declaring
that I was in the habit of paying for my own beefsteaks
when I ate them, and that I did not care particularly to
meet anyone that way.'bb   At Lucy's we have not yet

** Hardly true today, except in the most conservative circles. Brought up
in one of them myself I was going on thirty before I went walking alone
at night in New York. How exciting and delightful that first night walk
was – to an evening meeting of my Local School Board. Since then I
have been alone at night in various strange parts of the world, but that
first thrill of adventure I have never quite recovered.

bb I am reminded of the Bedouin women who require the stranger
whom they meet to set down whatever he has for them on the road a
few paces behind their backs. They take nothing from his hands.
Between them and the writer to the *Times* there is to be sure a
difference. The Bedouin women are not averse to asking for a present
of biscuit or flour. *E.C.P.*

cooked a beefsteak nor made bread, but we are quite casual about inviting in 'a man or two', or about not paying for the toast we eat or the tea we drink. And the other day when I opened the door to a man I had never seen before, I told him that he could come in only if he had brought some cigarettes with him, we all being at the moment destitute. No doubt our letter writer wouldn't stand for Lucy's. She would certainly not come a second time. On Morningside Heights she stuck it out for two months. Then she left. 'I think I should have gone mad if I hadn't', she writes. 'Evening after evening we spent sitting apart, she in her room and I in *mine*, with never a sound or word to break the mute antagonism that existed between us. But occasionally, after I had gone to bed, I heard the bell ring, and I knew she was entertaining a man visitor. I say nothing against this. She was lonely, too; but I, at least, could thank God that I was alone.' Perhaps others have thanked him too.... Such women are misfits.[cc] 'All we ask,' she goes on, 'for there must be thousands like me – is companionship of the right kind. We are not exacting. If the bond that unites us be not a very subtle one, still do we accept it gladly.' True, my dear young lady, you are not asking for much and you may get it for the asking in many parts of the world, but not, I thank God in my turn, in New York. The New Yorker has begun to be something more than merely gregarious, flocking strictly with his own kind and fleeing from anyone of a different status.

Newport, August 3.
My last entry I see is about four months old. How far away from it I've been. It was only this morning as I was

[cc] Quite true; they are as much out of place in a socially developing community like New York as Bedouin women would be. A Bedouin woman could not go in a street car because she could give nothing to a strange man nor take anything from him. What could she do about her fare? The lonely letter writer is not quite as restricted as far as the conductor is concerned; but suppose she happened to have forgotten her purse; would she, do you think, let the amiable gentleman who noticed her predicament pay her fare for her? Bedouin women are not lonely because like savage women everywhere they keep together by sex and age. Our letter writer asks for much the same arrangement. E.C.P.

sailing in the bay that I remembered this record. I was
listening to the lament of the yacht's mistress over the effect
of the European war on suffrage. They had had a great
publicity campaign in hand for the autumn, pages of
suffrage stuff for the Sunday newspapers, and now since
the war the papers would give them no space at all. And of
course nobody was interested at all in suffrage at present.
She was going to advise her Committee not to spend any
money; there were no ears for their propaganda. 'It is just
what happened to the Woman Movement during our Civil
War,' I commented, adding oracularly, 'One of the greatest
costs of war is the set back it gives to all advance
movements...'.[48] 'Besides women count for so little in war',
concluded my hostess. It was then I remembered this
record and why it had been so long neglected. I've been
living in a region of culture whereas in regions at war
feminism is aloof, and expressions of sex are too primitive
[elemental] to be recorded[dd] or even observed. Amos is
president of a coal company in the Queen Charlotte
Islands, British Columbia, and early in June he planned a
'vacation trip' to those parts. He invited me to go with him
and I accepted. We lived in the mining camps, we made a
timber cruise, we went on a wild cattle hunt. And the men

[dd] Primitive though they be, they are sometimes recorded. Part of the
directions Kitchener[49] had printed this summer for his soldiers reads as
follows: 'In this new experience you may find temptation both in wine
and women. You must entirely resist both temptations and while
treating women with perfect courtesy you should avoid any intimacy.'
E.C.P.

[48] The entry of the United States into the First World War split the
suffrage movement between those who, like Carrie Chapman Catt of
the National American Woman Suffrage Association, were willing to
engage in a limited amount of 'war work' to persuade the government
of their fitness to undertake the serious responsibility of voting, and
those who were both pro-suffrage and anti-militarist. Many of the
latter refused to compromise their principles on the issue by cooperating
with government war aims. The opportunities for women to perform
'war work' may indeed have supplied an impetus to the suffrage cause –
but it was a cause which was in any case steadily gaining ground even
before the outbreak of the war in Europe.

[49] Kitchener. Horatio Herbert, Earl Kitchener (1850–1916), British
general and colonial administrator.

with us were the usual miscellany of a pioneer country.... I
was 'the only woman' and I was treated as such, a creature
of quite another world, to be looked after very carefully, to
be given no charge or responsibility, all that was expected
of her being that she should not complain over much of
inevitable hardships or discomforts. It was rather lonely,
this distinction, until one day I found some one willing to
treat me like a fellow being. We had left the boats we were
poling up stream to lunch on the river bank. As I sat under
a yellow cedar of that wonderful virgin forest watching the
men broiling part of a salmon on a piece of tin stove cast
aside by an earlier river party, I thought of how different
the distribution of labor had been the last time I was
camping – in New Mexico – and I laughed. 'Why do you
laugh?' asked Amos. 'I'm thinking that if you all were
Indians I'd be broiling that salmon and you'd be looking
on.' The men glanced at me, their attention arrested, and
one of them had the grace and wit to say: 'Let's play
Indian.' Later when we were again in the boats in token of
gratitude I passed him back a cigarette that I had lit for him
in my holder, knowing his hands were wet; he was running
the gasoline engine that we used in the less shallow parts of
the stream. Presently I heard the man back of him poling
say in a rather loud, belligerent tone: 'Larry, what is it that
makes you so successful? Is it what you say or the way you
look?' Larry muttered and I bided my time. It came in
about half an hour when we grounded on a pebbly stretch
and every one in the boat took the opportunity for a
smoke. As I passed my cigarette case to McDougal, the
belligerent, I said: 'What is it, do you think, makes a
woman successful? Is it what she says or the way she
looks?' 'The way she looks', he answered, more belligerent
than ever. 'And there's no exception to that. The sex
would be a lot more attractive if they never spoke at all.'
Receiving no answer [to this] our modern Paul[50] went on in
a cantankerous rasping voice: 'That sounds as if I was a
married man, but I ain't guilty.' 'It sounds as if your

[50] 'modern Paul'. See note 35, above. See also Paul's Epistle to Timothy
2.11: 'Let the woman learn in silence with all subjection.'

acquaintance among women was limited,' I said to myself and afterwards in effect to Larry that evening when he was making me up a hemlock bed, but repartee at the moment would have been out of place.

Not only were his acquaintances, I fancy, limited; but his means of making them. He happened to have been on the same steamer with us the night we crossed over from Prince Rupert to Massett. On the little sound steamer was also a half breed Haida girl, a graduate of the government school at Fort Simpson. She was pretty, young, unsophisticated, but curiously talkative considering her Indian blood. We 'made friends'. 'Do you know that man?' and she pointed 'Paul' out to me as he stood on the other side of the deck. 'I hate him', she added. 'Last night he was polite to me at first and I answered politely, and then before I knew it he put his arms around me and tried to kiss me. 'You mustn't do that' I said to him. 'I couldn't help it', he answered. And so I just had to lock myself in my cabin. I hate him.' She really wasn't the squaw woman he took her for. Poor mistaken and mistake-making Paul, whether in Palestine or in the Queen Charlotte islands! And how entrenched in primitive circles the squaw-goddess theory is! Neither squaw nor goddess talks. Language is for men. Let women only look their part – squaw or goddess as it happens to be. The squaw works, the goddess idles; but neither is doing the same things men are doing.

It makes no difference in a pioneer country if the men are of different classes, of different education, of different traditions. Pioneering, they have the same work, they wear the same kind of clothes, they eat the same kind of food. It is on these comparatively superficial things their sense of fellowship rests. I wonder if to achieve fellowship with men women will not have to be in superficial ways more like them, particularly in dress. To be treated as [a] human being by the 'civilized world', it has undoubtedly been necessary for the Chinaman to cut off his pigtail. Won't women too have to cut off their pigtails? It is a pity that men's clothes just now are so very ugly. And yet the sacrifice in wearing them may inject just enough of the martyr spirit into the reform to carry it through.

August, Saratoga Springs.

Amos invited me to join him here for the Republican Convention – a convention which to the old timers must seem not a convention, for under the direct primary law they are making no nominations. In place of the pictures and proclamations of candidates are the banners and battle cries of the suffragists. The balconies of the hotel are draped with their flags, a flamboyant banner is even hung across the big court and placards at every turn direct you to their headquarters. As one steps off the train and passes under the high arched doorway of the hotel it has all the look of a suffrage convention. The suffragists want the Committee on Resolutions to report in favor of having their question not only submitted to the voters by the Constitutional Convention but favorably recommended as a plank in the Republican platform. [They plead that this much was promised them at the Republican convention of 1912. H. has told them that although the wording of the platform of that year is ambiguous the sense of the committee who framed it was not for suffrage. They disbelieve him, for they think the ambiguity of phrasing was a political trick. Nevertheless they have taken H. for their spokesman and abettor. He introduced their resolution upon the floor of the Convention.] At the hearing before the Committee on Resolutions Mrs Carrie Chapman Catt[51] and Mrs Blatch were heard for suffrage, Miss Chittenden against it. [Miss C is – of the – .] Mrs Catt was a link with the past. Abe was her protagonist and her speech was full of the echoes of the Women's Rights women of the Fifties. It seemed a curious bit of anachronism. Mrs Blatch by contrast was very modern, excessively modern at one point it seemed perhaps to more than one conservative man. The night before Horace White, some time lieutenant governor of New York and for a brief period governor, had made a public attack on Woman Suffrage, referring to women with the vote as 'a menace to government'. Over night Mrs Blatch had ascertained that while H.W. was governor he had used the

[51] Catt. See notes 38, 48, above.

gubernatorial prerogative to restore to the rights of citizenship over eighty ex-criminals, among them offenders against the election laws and several rapists. And so at the conclusion of her speech before the Committee on Resolutions in the hotel 'parlor' – that phantastic stretch of all enveloping sky-blue upholstery and gilt frames and fixtures – what does Mrs Blatch do but up and charge Horace White with the impropriety of defending the franchise against women, *he* the restorer of the franchise to eighty odd male criminals. Horace White met the attack by admitting the facts. Mrs Blatch had not been as inaccurate on this occasion, he remarked, as he had known her to be on others. Then he seemed to forget whatever else he had intended to say, for he unexpectedly sat down.... I was told afterwards by one of Mrs B's lieutenants that before the meeting Horace White had sent emissaries to her, having heard of her inquisition, to assure her that his action as governor had been perfectly proper and had had the support of an endless number of clergymen. The emissaries would have done better by him, I gathered from the scorn in the voice of my informant, if they had left out the clergymen.[ee] At any rate, they hadn't called off Mrs Blatch. 'Would a man have attacked the record of an opponent in that way?' I queried to Amos. 'Perhaps not,' he answered, 'but it was a good thing for her to have done. Next time Horace White will be more guarded in his anti-suffrage statements. He'll remember.' Yes, he'll remember, and the other men too who witnessed the controversy and who object to having their conventionalities ignored. 'I'm against woman suffrage', said old Senator B to me that very evening. 'Mrs Blatch is the most impudent woman I've ever known. Anyhow I'm against woman suffrage. I wouldn't encourage any woman to read *The Federalist* and anyhow the women I like don't want to read it. I'm entirely against woman suffrage...'. 'Why are *you* against woman suffrage, do you mind telling me?' I asked Miss Chittenden later on as we stood on the steps of the hotel

---

[ee] An omission hardly to be expected of them, however, knowing that women are peculiarly subject to the authority of the Church. *E.C.P.*

listening with the crowd in the street below to the cart tail
suffrage oratory. 'There are so many reasons, it's hard to
begin,' she began. 'But the chief,' I urged. 'The chief is that
it would weaken the government.'[ff] 'Oh,' I said, [much
enjoying this expression of the old 'collective representation' of the infection of feminine weakness]. 'What's
more,' Miss C went on, 'I'm more of an anti-suffragist since
I've been here at this convention than ever. I'm a pretty
strong woman, but it's worn me out. Women can't stand
the strain of politics. I'm going to bed. Good night.' 'Did
she convince you?' asked an old lady standing near me.
'Hardly', and we laughed together and the girl with the old
lady said, 'I'd like to know what difference it makes to the
question at what hour *she* has to go to bed...?' The street
meeting was disbanding, and as the suffragist cart drove off
two of the girls who had spoken from it passed me by,
calling out an invitation to go on with them to a dance at
the Grand Union Hotel. The affirmative side is always, I
suppose, more productive of energy than the negative.

Newport, August
On leaving Saratoga I was amused to find one of my
suffragist friends acting like 'any ordinary woman'. She
and I and Amos had been invited by a man with a motor to
motor down to New York City with him, rather a liberal
offer as he knew he would hear suffrage talk most of the
way and as he himself was enough anti-suffrage to declare
that if women had the vote he wouldn't want to be an
election district captain any longer.[gg] Not liking motoring I

[ff] The theory implicit in this 'collective representation', the theory of the
infection of feminine weakness, is very old. During the period of
initiation in their tribe Blackfellow lads believe that the touch or sight of
a woman or even the falling of her shadow upon them would bring
them illness or blindness or decrepitude, or make them lazy or stupid.
In the Barea tribe of East Africa husband and wife do not sleep together
for 'the breath of the wife weakens her husband'. The Melanesians of
New Guinea believe that if a woman were even to enter their clubhouse
it would very shortly burn down to the ground. E.C.P.

[gg] Cp. Parsons, *The Old-Fashioned Woman*, pp. 146–7, where I somewhat
frivolously suggested that some day men might be leaving politics to the
women. But the above declaration was made, I am told, in no frivolous
spirit. E.C.P.

accepted only as far as Albany, intending to make a close train connection there. We missed the connection and Amos suggested taking the train with me. 'Then I'll train too,' said the suffragist, 'I couldn't think of arriving so late in New York with only one man.' I laughed and of course arranged that she should arrive in New York with two men. Women will be women – in spite of suffrage. Or, let me tell you, Mr B – in spite of going in bathing with men. I sat next to Mr B at dinner last night. He is again this summer President of the Beach Association. He never goes in swimming himself; but he has views about swimming, particularly about men and women swimming together. 'When I was a boy,' he said, 'there were different hours for bathing on the beach for men and women. Now they not only go in the water together, but they sit together in their bathing clothes on the beach. What's to become of all the sentiment and mystery in life, I'd like to know. What's to become of all the poetry? It's just like animals.' 'So is eating', I came very near saying, as I watched him add one more dish to the many he had already partaken of. But I held my peace, and he changed the subject to tell me he thought the European war was a good cure for socialism.

Newport, August.
I went to New York yesterday to march in the Women's Peace Parade. I had written to the Secretary of its Committee urging that men be not excluded; but excluded or not there were no men in the parade. There were about 2000 women. We marched five in a line four feet from the woman ahead and four feet from the woman in [the same] line. It was a motley lot of women. Ahead of me was a girl who might have been a college student; behind was an East side Jewess, a factory girl perhaps. She carried a school globe draped in black and purple paper. There was fun in her eye and she no doubt enjoyed the hand clapping she from time to time provoked. Levity of any kind was far from the spirit of the woman on my left. She was of an obvious middle age, stout and florid, but her mouth was almost grim and she had worked so hard all her life, she

told me, that it made her mad to see so many idle people in the streets. Did she want to march to empty streets, I wondered. These were not empty, but were lined on both sides from two to four persons deep the whole length of our march, 56th Street to Union Square. It was a dumb, rather bewildered looking crowd, except for the jeering faces of the young men. But even the young men were not vociferous as was the wont of some of them in the suffrage parades. And yet if you were looking for the grotesque, how much more of it you could have had out of the Peace Parade! But then one must treat one primitive with another, and parading is not more primitive or more absurd than fighting. 'What effect do you expect your marching on Fifth Avenue to have on Emperor William?' asked Janet, swinging in the hammock. 'There's not much hope for him, he's too old,' I answered, 'but if there are any Hohenzollerns[52] on earth a hundred years from now, peace parading may have improved their position. But there are other reasons for it, my sceptical daughter.'

---

[52] Emperor William: Kaiser Wilhelm of Germany. Hohenzollerns: The German royal family.

SELECT BIBLIOGRAPHY

Selected works by Elsie Clews Parsons

'The Aversion to Anomalies'. *Journal of Philosophy, Psychology and Scientific Method*, 15 April 1915: pp. 212–19.

'Do You Believe in Patriotism?' *The Masses*, March 1916: p. 12.

The Educational Legislation and Administration of the Colonies. New York: Columbia University Press, 1899.

'Engagements'. *The Masses*, Nov. 1916: p. 14.

Facing Race Suicide'. *The Masses*, June 1915: p. 15.

The Family: An Ethnographical and Historical Outline. New York: Putnam's, 1906.

Fear and Conventionality. New York: Putnam's, 1914.

'Feminism and Conventionality'. *Women in Public Life: Annals of the American Academy of Politican and Social Science* 56 (1914): pp. 47–53.

'Feminism and Sex Ethics'. *International Journal of Ethics*, July 1916: pp. 462–65.

Folklore of the Sea Islands, South Carolina. New York: Stechert, 1923.

'How they are Voting'. *New Republic*, 21 Oct. 1940: p. 554.

'The Last Zuni Transvestite'. *American Anthropologist* 41 (1939): pp. 338–40.

'Marriage: A New Life'. *The Masses*, Sept. 1916: pp. 27–28.

'Marriage and Parenthood: A Distinction.' *International Journal of Ethics* 25 (1915): pp. 514–17.

The Old-Fashioned Woman: Primitive Fancies about the Sex. 1913. New York: Arno Press, 1972.

'On the Loose'. *New Republic*, 27 Feb. 1915: pp. 100–101.

'A Pacifist Patriot'. *The Dial*, Mar. 1920: pp. 367–70.

'Patterns for Peace or War'. *Scientific Monthly*, Sept. 1917: pp. 229–38.

'Penalizing Marriage and Child-Bearing.' *The Independent*, 18 Jan. 1906: pp. 146–47.

A Pueblo Indian Journal, 1920–1921. Menasha, Wisconsin: American Anthropological Association, 1925, No. 32.

Pueblo Indian Religion. 1939. Chicago: Midway Reprints, University of Chicago Press, 1974.

Religious Chastity: An Ethnological Study. 1913. (Pseudonym John Main.) New York: AMS Press, 1975.

Social Freedom: A Study of the Conflicts Between Social Classifications and Personality. New York: Putnam's, 1915.

Social Rule: A Study of the Will to Power. New York: Putnam's, 1916.

'The Study of Variants'. *Journal of American Folklore* April–June 1920: pp. 87–90.

'The Supernatural Policing of Women'. *The Independent*, 8 Feb. 1912: pp. 307–10.

'The Teleological Delusion'. *Journal of Philosophy, Psychology and Scientific Method*, Aug. 1917: pp. 463–68.

'Waiyautitsa of Zuni, New Mexico'. *Scientific Monthly*, Nov. 1919: pp. 443–57.

'When Mating and Parenthood are Theoretically Distinguished'. *International Journal of Ethics* 26 (1916): pp. 207–16.

Biographies of Elsie Clews Parsons

Boas, Franz. 'Elsie Clews Parsons'. *Science*, 23 Jan. 1942: pp. 89–90.

Bourne, Randolph. 'A Modern Mind'. *The Dial*, 62 (1917): pp. 239–40.

Day, Clarence. 'Portrait of a Lady'. *New Republic*, 23 (1919): pp. 387–89.

Hare, Peter. *A Woman's Quest for Science: Portrait of Anthropologist Elsie Clews Parsons*. Buffalo, New York: Prometheus, 1985.

Kroeber, Alfred Louis. 'Elsie Clews Parsons'. *American Anthropologist* 45 (1943): p. 252.

Sicherman, Barbara, et al. *Notable American Women: The Modern Period*. Cambridge, Massachusetts: Belknap, 1980.

Zumwalt, Rosemary Levy. *Wealth and Rebellion: Elsie Clews Parsons, Anthropologist and Folklorist*. Urbana and Chicago: University of Illinois Press, 1992.

Works containing biographical notes on Parsons

Caffrey, Margaret M. *Ruth Benedict: Stranger in this Land*. Austin: University of Texas Press, 1989.

Jones, Margaret C. *Heretics and Hellraisers: Women Contributors to 'The Masses', 1911–1917*. Austin: University of Texas Press, 1993.

O'Neill, William L. *Echoes of Revolt: 'The Masses', 1911–1917*. Chicago: Quadrangle, 1966.

Rudnick, Lois Palken. *Mabel Dodge Luhan: New Woman, New Worlds*. Albuquerque, New Mexico: University of New Mexico Press, 1984.

Sandeen, Eric. 'Bourne Again: the Correspondence Between Randolph Bourne and Elsie Clews Parsons'. *American Literary History*, Fall 1989: pp. 489–509.

Sanger, Margaret. *Autobiography.* New York: Norton, 1938.

Schwartz, Judith. *Radical Feminists of Heterodoxy: Greenwich Village 1912–1940.* Lebanon, New Hampshire: New Victoria Publishers, 1982.

Other works cited

Borrow, George. *Lavengro.* 1851. London: Murray, 1888.

Brieux, Eugène. *Three Plays by Brieux.* Ed. George Bernard Shaw. London: Fifield, 1911.

Byron, George Gordon. *Don Juan.* Ed. Isaac Asimov. Garden City, New York: Doubleday, 1972.

Catullus, Gaius Valerius. Transl. F.W. Cornish. In *Catullus, Tibullus and Pervigilium Veneris.* London: Heinemann, 1988.

Cott, Nancy. *The Grounding of Modern Feminism.* New Haven, Connecticut: Yale University Press, 1987.

Dorr, Rheta Childe. *What Eight Million Women Want.* Boston: Small, 1910.

Godwin, William. *Collected Novels and Memoirs.* Ed. Mark Philip. London: Pickering, 1992.

Key, Ellen. *The Century of the Child.* New York: Putnam's, 1909.

Lévy-Bruhl, Lucien. *How Natives Think (Les fonctions mentales dans les sociétiés inférieures. 1910).* New York: Washington Square Press, 1966.

Luhan, Mabel Dodge. *Movers and Shakers.* 1936. Albuquerque, New York: University of New Mexico Press, 1985.

Meynell, Alice. *Prose and Poetry.* Ed. Victoria Sackville-West, et al. London: Cape, 1947.

Miller, Alice Duer. *Are Women People?* New York: Doran, 1915.

Vorse, Mary Heaton. *A Footnote to Folly: the Reminiscences of Mary Heaton Vorse.* New York: Farrar, 1935.

Wells, H.G. *The Passionate Friends.* London: Newnes, 1917.